'Diverting and disquieting . . . as might be expected from a writer of John Boyne's reputation, the collection is never less than inventive and extremely readable'
Irish Times

'John Boyne confirms his pla[...] rising literary stars with this [...] of stories . . . At its best – as in the justly award-winning story "Rest Day" – Boyne offers writing of insight and beauty that elevates this collection to impressive heights indeed'
Observer

'The best of the best . . . These revealing stories, unfolding like intimate confessions, will twist your heart'
Daily Mail

'Boyne has achieved a careful authenticity . . . Boyne's *Beneath the Earth* is a satisfying and polished set of short stories with definite longevity and immense global appeal'
Irish Independent

'Boyne is particularly strong on dramatising child and teen sensibilities but here we see how the badness of adults spills over and infects these damaged children'
Independent

'Each one is like a novel in microcosm, and all tw[...]
of the
Irish [...]

JOHN BOYNE'S NOVELS

A History of Loneliness (2014)

'Gripping, harrowing and extremely moving . . .
A painfully page-turning read . . . A vividly three-
dimensional dissection of both the priesthood and
the larger cultural malaise of Ireland'
Sunday Times

This House is Haunted (2013)

'A lesson in classic storytelling . . . [Boyne] takes us
on a highly original, entertaining journey that, like
all great ghost stories, saves its most unexpected twist
for the very end'
Sunday Independent

The Absolutist (2011)

'A novel of immeasurable sadness, in a league with
Graham Greene's *The End of the Affair*. John Boyne
is very, very good at portraying the destructive power
of a painfully kept secret'
John Irving

The House of Special Purpose (2009)

'A tour de force, at once epic and intimate, and above
all a marvellous read'
John Banville

Mutiny on the Bounty (2008)

'Storytelling at its most accomplished. Bears comparison with William Golding's *Rites of Passage*'
Independent

Next of Kin (2006)

'A moving and insightful book . . . stylistically fluent and engages the reader with every word'.
Irish Independent

Crippen (2004)

'Engaging . . . keeps the reader on the edge of their seat'
Irish Times

The Congress of Rough Riders (2001)

'A total blast . . . clever, provocative stuff. A formidable achievement'
Independent

The Thief of Time (2000)

'An extraordinary debut'
Sunday Express

HIS NOVELS FOR YOUNGER READERS

The Boy at the Top of the Mountain (2015)

'There is a sureness and a simplicity to the writing that is very impressive . . . In *The Boy at the Top of the Mountain*, Boyne has delivered a powerful account of how one boy was seduced by Hitler and Nazism and paid the price'
Irish Independent

Stay Where You Are And Then Leave (2013)

'A work of tender beauty and real lives . . . an instant classic . . . John Boyne has recreated a world that deserves to be remembered forever'
Eoin Colfer, author of the *Artemis Fowl* series

The Terrible Thing That Happened To Barnaby Brocket (2012)

'Unashamedly and often delightfully whimsical . . . It has much of the pell-mell what-the-hell-happens-nextness of Dahl and Ibbotson'
Guardian

Noah Barleywater Runs Away (2010)

'Timeless and imaginative. I don't know how Boyne does it but his story is incredibly resonant'
Irish Times

The Boy in the Striped Pyjamas (2006)

'It's a great book, energetic, vivid, and amazing in the scope of its appeal. In the space of three days it had been read, and loved, by everybody in my house. The dog felt left out'
Roddy Doyle

By John Boyne

NOVELS

The Thief of Time
The Congress of Rough Riders
Crippen
Next of Kin
Mutiny on the Bounty
The House of Special Purpose
The Absolutist
This House Is Haunted
A History of Loneliness

NOVELS FOR YOUNGER READERS

The Boy in the Striped Pyjamas
Noah Barleywater Runs Away
The Terrible Thing That Happened to Barnaby
Brocket
Stay Where You Are and Then Leave
The Boy at the Top of the Mountain

NOVELLAS

The Second Child
The Dare

SHORT STORIES

Beneath the Earth

For more information on John Boyne and his books,
see his website at www.johnboyne.com

Beneath the Earth

Stories

John Boyne

BLACK SWAN

TRANSWORLD PUBLISHERS
61–63 Uxbridge Road, London W5 5SA
www.transworldbooks.co.uk

Transworld is part of the Penguin Random House group of companies
whose addresses can be found at global.penguinrandomhouse.com

Penguin
Random House
UK

First published in Great Britain in 2015 by Doubleday
an imprint of Transworld Publishers
Black Swan edition published 2016

Some of these stories originally appeared elsewhere, in slightly different forms:
'Rest Day' in *The Irish Times*; 'Araby' in *Dubliners 100*; 'Empire Tour' in *The
Moth*; 'The Vespa' in *Books Ireland*; 'The Country You Called Home' in *The
Great War*; 'Beneath The Earth' in *The Penny Dreadful*.

A CIP catalogue record for this book
is available from the British Library.

ISBN
9781784160999

Typeset in Giovanni Book by Kestrel Data, Exeter, Devon.
Printed and bound by Clays Ltd, Bungay, Suffolk.

Penguin Random House is committed to a sustainable
future for our business, our readers and our planet. This book is made from
Forest Stewardship Council® certified paper.

MIX
Paper from
responsible sources
FSC® C018179

1 3 5 7 9 10 8 6 4 2

for Simon Trewin

Contents

Boy, 19

I started charging for sex a few days after my nineteenth birthday. I recognized my body for what it was: an asset that could be rented to the lonely for an hour at a time. There's no shortage of damaged men in Dublin who want to lavish attention on the boy they weren't allowed to love when they were young and I knew that they would like me.

The idea came about through a combination of necessity and happenstance. Although my scholarship paid my tuition fees, it did not cover living expenses and I found myself sharing a house with three students who nauseated me. They spent their evenings watching television together, noisily eating takeaway food and making derogatory comments about girls they wanted to fuck but who did not want to fuck them. To share a living space with them made me feel diminished as a person. One evening I was making my way down Bachelors Walk when I stopped to light a cigarette. As I leaned back against a doorway, wondering where I might go to avoid that squalid flat, a much older man approached me. He smiled as if we were old friends and called me 'mate'.

He asked how I was doing. I told him I was doing fine. He asked whether I was waiting for someone. I told him no. He said he didn't want anything unusual, just a bit of fun, and I stared at him, confused, before walking on. I was halfway home before I realized what he'd meant. And then I regretted not asking him how much money he had.

I'm lucky. I live in the age of the Internet. The next morning I spent less than a minute on Google before I found an appropriate website to advertise my services. I stood in front of a mirror with my shirt off, wearing a low-slung pair of jeans, and took a photograph. I didn't show my face entirely; the picture started just beneath my eyes and ended at my knees. It was clear enough to show what was on offer, obscure enough that no one would recognize me. I listed the things I was willing to do, which were many things, and the things I was unwilling to do, which were few. I checked the other ads and positioned myself within an appropriate price range. My age meant that I could charge more. It would be almost a year before my price would need to drop. I saved the ad, went into town to buy a second phone – a cheap one – and a new SIM card. I listed the number on the ad. I posted the ad. The phone rang that night. Four times.

I was nervous my first time but the man I chose was polite and self-conscious when he called, which reassured me. I took a shower and was surprised to notice that I was somewhat aroused. I wasn't looking forward to it but I wasn't dreading it either. He lived in Ranelagh. I made my way there and knocked on his door. He opened it wearing a pair of slacks, a shirt, a cardigan and an apron. He told me that he'd been cooking and asked whether I was hungry. I said I was and he said he could make me a bacon sandwich if I liked. Tick-tock, I said. One hour. Feed me if you want, but tick-tock. He turned off the oven, put the bacon back in the fridge and removed his apron.

He asked me to sit on the sofa and I did. The television was on. *Coronation Street*. Behind a newsagent's counter, a woman with a helmet of red hair was teasing her colleague. It was quite amusing. The man asked my name and I told him. The name on my ad, not my real name. He asked whether I was really nineteen and I said that I was. He asked did I get lonely sometimes, like he did. Tick-tock, I said. He nodded and started to undo my belt. I noticed a photograph on the mantlepiece of the man, many years younger, with two people I took to be his parents and who looked kind and loving.

It was a good start for me. He didn't remove any of his clothes, nor did he want me to touch him. He didn't ask me to undress. All he wanted was to blow me, which he did. I lay my head back on the sofa and tried to clear my mind. A small dog wandered into the room and sat on his hind legs, observing us. The man's mobile phone rang and he ignored it. I came in his mouth; he didn't pull away or complain. It wasn't unpleasurable. Afterwards, he went to the sink and poured a glass of water, gargled with it and spat it out. He handed me five twenty-euro notes and didn't look at me again.

You have my number, I told him, but he didn't reply.

He put his apron back on and took the bacon out of the fridge. I patted the dog. I took the bus home and started looking at flats that I might soon be able to afford on my own. I showered again, then slept soundly. The next morning I lodged the hundred euros in my account, which was overdrawn at the time. It would never be overdrawn again.

Rachel started drinking when I was thirteen, the same year Peter left. Rachel is my mother; Peter is my father. A few months earlier, my sister was killed when she was walking home from school. She ran across a road without looking and a car hit her. She was on life support for two weeks. Rachel and Peter argued over whether they should switch the machine off. Then she died anyway.

Rachel and Peter stopped pretending to love each other after that. I came home from school and Rachel told me that we were having spaghetti bolognese for dinner. She told me to clean my room and throw my clothes in the washing machine. She told me that Peter had moved out. She told me she was going out with the girls that night. Fine, I said.

She stopped putting food in the fridge and started putting bottles of wine in there instead. She told me a little glass in the evening kept her sane. She drank two bottles a day. Then three. She asked me did I want some. We sat together playing card games in the evening and she said she really shouldn't be doing this but that she'd prefer that I was sitting in the kitchen drinking with her than out somewhere drinking with my friends. I told her they wouldn't be out drinking anyway, that they were only children, like me. She refilled my glass.

On bad nights, she would look at photographs of my sister and cry as she drank. She told me she felt lonely. She said she couldn't be alone. She knocked on my bedroom door and said that she needed me with her. She said she wanted to keep me safe. She slept in the bed with me and wrapped her body around me. She turned me around to face her and held me closer. She said that no one would ever love me like my mother would. She said she wanted to show me how much she loved me.

I started going into school with hangovers and one of my teachers grew concerned. I was called into the form tutor's office for a meeting. How is everything at home, he asked me. Fine, I said. It was a terrible thing that happened to your sister, he said. She's with God now, I said. That she is, that she is, he said, taking off his glasses, peering through the lenses and cleaning them with his soiled handkerchief before putting them back on. And how are your parents, he asked me. I told him that Peter had moved out. Who is Peter, he asked me. My father, I told him. You call your father Peter, he asked me. I do, I told him. Isn't that quite unusual, he asked me. I suppose, I told him. Does he not want you to call him Daddy, he asked me. No, I told him. And what about your mother, he asked me. Rachel, I said. You call your mother Rachel, he asked me. I do, I told him. I never heard of such a thing, he said. Is your mammy taking care of you, he asked me. Rachel, I said. Is Rachel taking care of you, he asked me. No one will ever love me like my mother does, I told him. We're concerned about you, he said. Your teachers, I mean. You seem tired in the mornings. And your eyes are red. And quite frankly, there's a smell of alcohol about you, as if you've been drinking. That's because I've been drinking, I told him. You've been drinking, he said. Yes, I told him. What do you drink, he asked me. I drink white wine, I told him. Cheap stuff. It goes down smooth but comes out rocky. He stared at me and said nothing for a long time. Does your mother know that you drink, he asked me. Do you mean Rachel, I said. Does Rachel know that you drink, he asked me. She's the one who pours it out for me, I told him. Your mother gives you drink, he said, more of a statement than a question. Rachel gives me drink, I told him. All right then, he said, you go on back to your class, there's a good boy. Let me have a think about this. And I went back to my class, where I felt tired. I was looking forward to getting home. I had a thirst on me. It had started coming on me every day at this time.

When the bell rang, a man and a woman were waiting for me outside the classroom. We're going to take you home today, they told me. We'd like a word with your mother. Fine, I said. They drove me home in a red Cortina. Rachel was lying on the sofa watching television. She had a hand down the front of her tracksuit pants. She stood up when the man and the woman came in, unsteady on her feet. There were wine bottles on the floor. Who have you been talking to, you little shit, asked Rachel, advancing on me, and the woman stood between us. I'll make the call, said the man, taking a phone from his pocket and stepping out into the hallway.

I was told to pack a bag and a couple of hours later I found myself in a house near Dartmouth Square with a couple named George and Sarah Day, and their son Eugene, who offered me a game of Monopoly. I was told I was to stay with the Days until a decision was made about me.

Fine, I said.

I always say you have my number when I leave someone's house but it's unusual for a man to call me twice. Perhaps I'm not good at my job. It's a possibility, of course, but I do try to give value for money. I think it's more likely that men don't want me to remember them. If I see them more than once, then I might recognize them as they walk down Grafton Street, holding their children by the hands as they look into the Christmas window at Brown Thomas. Or maybe they think that if they become familiar to me, I will blackmail them. Or, I suppose, murder them. But these are the things that happen in films, not in real life. I would never acknowledge a client on the street. Nor would I blackmail one. Nor would I commit a violent crime. I know this in my heart. But of course they do not, for they don't know me at all.

There is one couple, however, that I have seen several times. They are both in their fifties. Roger has a strong Galway accent; Jim tells me that he is Glaswegian. Roger and Jim live together off Parnell Square. They own an extraordinary amount of DVD films, which they shelve alphabetically on beautifully constructed shelves. Roger is visibly excited whenever I appear and undresses me quickly, his mouth on every part of my body. There is no small talk. Jim holds back and seems embarrassed to be part of this. He looks away when Roger kisses me. I can see that he hates where their life has led them, this intrusion of a young boy into their bedroom. I am certainly not the first; I will not be the last. When Roger is finished with me, he lies back and says *fuck* over and over in a tone that suggests that we have both been overwhelmed by the encounter. Jim looks away and gathers up my clothes for me, gives me my money. He asks me whether I would like to use their shower. I wash myself thoroughly before going downstairs even though I will shower again when I get home. By now, Roger is seated on the sofa wearing a faded dressing gown and flicking through the television channels. He never looks at me then.

The last time I left their house Jim walked me to the front door. Do you live far away, he asked me, and I shook my head. Not too far, I said. Do you mind if I ask what you do, he said. When you're not doing this, I mean. Of course you don't have to say if it makes you uncomfortable. If I tell you, will you tell Roger, I asked him. No, he said. I'm a student, I told him. He seemed disappointed by my reply. He thought I was lying. I wasn't lying. He put a hand on my shoulder and said that if Roger called again, would I mind saying that I was busy? He said that he knew this would cost me money but that he would be happy to make this good. He would give me one hundred euros for every time I said no to Roger. I shook my head and said that I would never come to their house again. That if Roger phoned me, I would not answer. But he'll call someone else, I told him, you know that, don't you? Yes, I know that, he said.

I wanted to stay with the Days but I couldn't. They were a halfway house, a place for boys like me to go in an emergency situation. Sarah was kind and efficient but her job was to prepare me for wherever I was going next. George talked to me about football. I didn't understand; he didn't care. He kept trying. Eugene didn't seem to mind having another boy in the house. He confided in me that he wanted to be a priest, a strange profession for someone our age. He said that he felt a calling inside him. Sarah and George Day asked me whether I wanted to talk about Rachel and Peter and I told them no, that I didn't.

I knew from my social worker that Rachel had been brought to a clinic where she was being treated for alcoholism. After that she was brought to a second clinic, where she was treated for depression. My social worker said that my sister's death had affected Rachel badly. She asked me whether I understood about Peter. Understood what, I asked. It doesn't matter, she said, consulting her file. Understood what, I asked again. I'm sorry, I spoke out of turn, she told me. Rachel is in hospital, my social worker told me. She has a long road to recovery. Would you like to see her, she asked me. No, I said. My social worker told me that was probably for the best, as Rachel wasn't emotionally equipped for visitors yet. Then we're all happy, I said.

I asked Sarah Day whether I could stay with her, George and Eugene, and she shook her head. You know that you can't, she told me.

I was brought to a house in Drumcondra to live with a family whose name was Grace. There was another foster child there, an angry girl named Chloe who refused to talk to me. My new foster parents took no interest in either of us. They had a son, Francis, nine years old, who did nothing but play video games and told me that I was there so the state would pay the mortgage. He pretended that I didn't exist, even though we shared a bedroom.

I excelled, however, in school. I was naturally gifted. My teachers took a particular interest in me. I overheard my English teacher telling my mathematics teacher that I had a tragic back-story, as if I was a character in a novel. I sat quietly in class, I did my homework, I answered questions politely. And of course I was good-looking, and adults prefer attractive children. Even if they are not looking at them with sexual thoughts in their mind, I noticed how the teachers were instinctively drawn to the attractive boys and girls. They sought our approval. They wanted us to like them.

The possibility of a scholarship was raised with me. There were certain grades that I needed to achieve. I felt certain that if I studied hard, I would achieve what my invigilators required. I succeeded. At my school graduation the headmaster brought me on to the stage, clutched my arm and declared me a triumph over adversity. The parents applauded. I felt nothing. A reception was held afterwards – tepid soft drinks and supermarket party food. On the way home I made my way through a park where two boys accosted me, asked me whether I had money, told me they wanted whatever I had. I fought them and hurt them.

A woman phoned. Do you meet women as well as men, she asked me. Yes, I said, even though I never had. There was a long pause. I could hear her breathing. I'm lonely, she said eventually. They're all fucking lonely. Yes, I said. Are you clean, she asked me.

She didn't want me to come to her home. She said she'd book a room in a hotel where the elevators didn't require a key card and I could come straight up.

I followed the corridor around to her room. I knocked on the door. I could hear her standing on the other side. I waited. She opened the door. Hello, she said.

She was wearing a heavy white bathrobe, the kind you only find in hotels, and smelled of bath salts. I could see steam on the mirror of the bathroom through the open door and knew that she had prepared herself for me. I feel ridiculous, she told me. Don't, I said. I've never done something like this before, she told me. I have, I said.

She sat down on the bed. She was trembling. I felt irritated. She should have come to terms with her decision before calling me. She beckoned me over and asked me to sit next to her. She stroked my face and ran a hand through my hair. She kissed me. Her mouth tasted of white wine. I thought of Rachel. She took my hand and placed it inside her bathrobe. My hand settled on her right breast. My fingers reached underneath to cup it.

Her head moved slowly back and she closed her eyes. She moaned a little, a sound filled with a mixture of despair, shame and longing. I felt no excitement. I worried that I would not be able to perform.

She lay back on the bed and asked me to take my shirt off. She loosened her bathrobe and I understood that she wanted me to help her untie the knot. When it came apart I stared at her body for a few moments before looking at her face again. Whatever unhappiness had brought her here, she was very beautiful. I began to feel aroused on a purely physical level. I stood up, undressed and began. She did not, I think, enjoy it very much. She was too nervous. She was on the edge of excitement but could not quite bring herself there. I ran my tongue across the indentation on the fourth finger of her left hand and she pulled away, shaking her head. Don't be cruel, she said.

Afterwards, she didn't invite me to take a shower. She went into the bathroom while I dressed and only when I knocked to say that I was leaving did she come out. She had been crying. She handed me my money. You have my number, I told her and left. I went for a beer in a nearby bar where I saw a boy from my schooldays sitting in the corner with his arm around a girl. Once, several years before, he had approached me at a party and told me that I had beautiful eyes.

I met a girl and tried to like her. She worked in a café I often visited. She told me she was from Hiroshima. I didn't know people still lived there, I said. Oh yes, she told me. Has your family lived there a long time, I asked her. No, she said. Her parents were both from a city called Masuda in the Shimane Prefecture. But they moved to Hiroshima in the 1980s after their marriage. I was intrigued by this idea. I asked her would she like to come for a walk with me some evening and she said yes.

I'm not accustomed to dating. I'm not even accustomed to sex, outside of my job. I have no interest in it. The boys in my class at the university talk of little else, perhaps because they get so little. The girls hold back, not for moral reasons but because they enjoy the power they have over the boys. I can understand this. Feeling desired can be a very potent force.

The girl's name was Hamako, which, she told me, meant child of the shore. She had come to Ireland to study medicine but discovered quite early on that she had no aptitude for the subject. She was frightened by the cadavers. She hated the smell of formaldehyde. She didn't care for blood. She wasn't even particularly interested in helping people. She said that she couldn't tell her parents she had left the course because they would be furious with her and insist that she return home.

Don't you like Japan, I asked her. No, she told me. It took me years to escape. I'm never going back. But what will you do, I asked her. What I am doing, she said. I can waitress for a year or two, save some money, then move somewhere else. Anywhere that isn't Japan.

The third time we went out, she took me to the beach in Killiney. I'd never been before but she came regularly. She knew a family who lived nearby and twice a week she would take their dogs for a long walk. Why can't they

27

walk their dogs themselves, I asked her. They're too busy, she said. Besides, it's easy money for me. We called on the family and for a moment I thought I recognized the man who opened the door but I was wrong. I'd never seen him before. He seemed pleased that Hamako had a boyfriend, even though I was not her boyfriend. He asked me many intimate questions about my family life and my studies at the university. His wife forced me to eat a slice of shop-bought cake and drink a cup of herbal tea that tasted like flowers. Their house was decorated with Japanese art and furniture. There were ink paintings on the walls featuring women in black and white kimonos, their hair held up with combs and pins, and a woodblock print of two kabuki actors performing before an audience of skeletons. Hamako didn't seem to want to leave, nor did she show any interest in taking the dogs for a walk.

Have you heard Hamako play the piano, the man asked me, and I shook my head. Oh no, don't ask me to, said Hamako in the kind of voice that made me realize that this was one of the reasons we were still here. Ask her to play, the man said to me. She can play if she wants to, I said. I'll play, said Hamako quickly, and she sat down before it, raised the lid and did some finger exercises in the air before starting. She was adequate, nothing more, but the man and woman applauded enthusiastically at the end. Isn't she wonderful, they asked me. They watched her as if she was their own child. She could do no wrong. I looked around and saw that there were no pictures of children to be seen anywhere. They asked me whether I could play a musical instrument and I shook my head. They asked if I could visit any city in the world, which one would I choose. I stopped talking. Another hour passed. I was invited to stay for dinner. I stood up and left.

When I returned home, I found a message waiting for me on my voicemail from Hamako telling me that she had never been so embarrassed in her life, that she had brought me to meet people who were important to her and I had behaved abominably. She said she wasn't sure if she wanted to see me again and that she would have to give it serious thought. She told me not to contact her again, that if she wanted to talk to me then she would be in touch. I deleted the message. She texted a few hours later in an advanced state of outrage and once again told me not to contact her. I deleted the message. When I woke the next morning, there were two messages, both quite abusive, and a third arrived during the day. I threw away the SIM card and bought a new one. It wasn't my work phone so it didn't matter and very few people had the number. Only my former social workers, who called me occasionally, and I informed them of the change.

I stopped frequenting Hamako's café and months later, when I thought enough time had passed that I could eat there again, she was nowhere to be seen. I asked what had become of her but the waitress who served me didn't know. Perhaps she had gone travelling after all. Or perhaps she'd returned to Japan.

Sometimes men phone, then hang up. Ten minutes pass, then they phone again. Their confidence has built up.

Maybe they've written down what they're going to say. I saw your profile online, they tell me. Are you available tonight? What time are you thinking of, I ask. As soon as you can make it, they say. They don't want to wait. They're in the mood, they have the urge, they hate themselves for it. They just want to do it so they can get on with their night. That's when they call me. Or boys like me.

Sometimes they block their number and when I answer, before they can say a word, I tell them to call back with an unblocked number. And then I hang up. Sometimes they call back. Sometimes they don't.

They might ask if I know someone I can bring with me. No, I tell them. There's no one you can call, they say. No. There's plenty of other lads online, they say, I thought you might all know each other. No. There's a long pause. So you don't know anyone, they say. No. All right, they say, come on your own. And I go on my own.

Only once did I go with someone else. Or rather there was someone else there when I arrived. This was in the early days. I couldn't have been doing it more than a few weeks. The boy was younger than me, maybe sixteen years old. Wild-eyed, probably on drugs. I came in and he was sitting on the sofa with his pants around his ankles. He barely looked up at me. His eyes were locked on a cat that was stretched out before an open fireplace, purring with contentment. Sit beside him, the man said. I sat beside him. Put your mouth on him, the man said. I put my mouth on him. Hit him, the man said, and I was going to say no but he must have been speaking to the boy because he roused himself, slapped me hard across the face and I fell off the sofa in surprise. I stood up and walked over to the man. Give me my money, I told him. But you haven't done anything yet, he said. I have so many ideas for the two of you. You're both so beautiful. Give me my money, I repeated, staring directly at him. He gave me my money. I left. I saw the boy another time near the canals in Baggot Street.

Sometimes they like to abuse me, verbally. They tell me how dirty I am. They say that I'm a nasty little scumbag. They tell me that I love it, the things that I do, and usually, when they're dribbling their bitterness, I'm thinking about an exam I have to take or whether I have enough milk in the fridge for breakfast. You're a disgusting fucking whore, they tell me. A filthy little cocksucker who takes it up the ass. You like the taste of it, don't you. I do, I tell them. I don't care. I'll say whatever they want me to say. It means nothing to me.

Once, I told someone. A boy from my class at the university who was gay and who'd made it clear that he was attracted to me. We were spending too much time together but it's not often that I make a friend. He asked me whether I had a girlfriend and I told him I wasn't interested in girls. I could see the desire in his eyes and didn't want to lose him. I didn't want to hurt him either. I considered sleeping with him, just to make him happy, but I don't do that for free. I told him how I made my living and he must have thought I was joking because he started laughing. I shrugged, looked away, and he sat back with a frown on his face. Are you serious, he asked me. I am, I told him. I'm not going to pay you, he said, offended. I never asked you to, I said. You've been leading me on, he said. I haven't, I told him. I like you. But he stopped liking me after that, which was probably easier for both of us.

Another time, I got a call from a man who grew aggressive when I said that I wouldn't be able to be there for an hour, maybe a little longer. Can you not come sooner, he asked, as if I should be at his beck and call. His voice was familiar to me. I thought maybe he'd called me before. I can't, I told him. I can be there in an hour, maybe a little longer. Well try, will you, he said. I waited an hour, maybe a little longer, and then I showed up. I rang the buzzer for his apartment on the outside wall. He lived in a good part of the city, a part I often find myself visiting. He kept me waiting in the cold. There was a camera above the buzzer and I put my finger across it. I didn't want him looking at me when I couldn't see him too. Finally, he answered. Another five seconds and I would have walked. Who's that, he said. It's me. About fucking time, he said. The door buzzed and I thought about going home. I had a bad feeling about this. I prefer nervous men to angry men. I went up a flight of stairs, then another, then another. I found the door. I put my finger across the spyhole. I knocked. He kept me waiting again. He opened it and looked at me. Jesus fucking Christ, he said, putting a hand across his mouth in shock. I started laughing. I'll leave you alone, Peter, I said. I walked away. I went home. I wiped his number.

Once, I took a beating. It was a young guy who called me. Twenty-two, twenty-three years old. There were three others waiting in another room and they set upon me. They pulled my pants down and poured lighter fluid on my cock and balls, then lit a match and held it in the air. They called me a dirty little faggot. Why are you doing this, I asked them. You know why, they said. But I didn't know why. I started to cry. They held the match closer. It went out and they lit another. When it burned out, they started hitting me. They didn't set me on fire. They let me go. I went home.

I received a call to tell me that Rachel wanted to see me. It had been more than six years since we'd last spoken and I wasn't sure that there were any ties left between us. My social workers asked me why I felt such anger towards her. They told me that she had a disease and that she could not be held responsible for it. I told them that I felt no anger towards her. Of course, they didn't know everything that had happened between us.

I asked whether Rachel was still in hospital and they told me no, that she had been an outpatient for a couple of years but only now felt ready to rebuild her relationship with me. Is she back in our old house, I asked, and they told me that Peter had sold the house long ago. It was his to sell, they said. Your mother has a flat in a new development off Pearse Street now. She gets a rent allowance from the state. How much did Peter get for the house, I asked, but they said they didn't know.

I brought a bunch of flowers when I visited. She opened the door and started to cry and I felt an unexpected emotion building inside me. I rarely feel things, so this was a surprise to me. She pulled me to her and hugged me tightly. Knowing that she would appreciate the gesture and that it would cost me nothing, I hugged her back. She let her head rest on my shoulder. I could feel her lips against my neck and pulled away.

You've grown tall, she said. And so handsome. You were just a boy when I saw you last. I'm still a boy, I told her. No, you're a man, she said. No, I said. No, no, I'm not. How are your studies going, she asked, and I told her that I had just completed an important set of exams and come fourth in my class. You were always so intelligent, she told me. I still can't believe that a son of mine goes to university. You're the first in our family ever to go there. I don't know where you get your brains from. It wasn't from your father or me, that's for sure. Do you know what you're going to be when you grow up, she asked. I thought of things the other students in my year said and decided to repeat their lines. I'd like to travel, I told her. I'd like to make a difference. I'd like to contribute to society in some meaningful way. I'd like to be an artist. I'd like to write a novel. I'd like to hike the Santiago de Compostela. I'd like to build houses in Africa. I'd like to meet someone who really understands me. I'd like to work for a non-profit. I'd like to be rich. I'd like to get on the property ladder. I'd like to have a job that gives me a clothing allowance. I'd like to effect real change in the places that matter. I'd like to help those who need help.

And you'll do all those things, she told me. With your

brains, you can do anything you want to do, be anything you want to be. Thanks, I told her. I didn't want to do any of those things, of course. But it made me feel normal to say them aloud.

She made two cups of tea and put too much milk in mine. She offered me a slice of cake, home-made, but I said no. You need to eat, she said. There's not a pick on you. Did you miss me, she asked. While I was away, did you miss me, did you think of me? I thought of you every day, I said, even though I hadn't, for I felt no urge to be cruel to her. I suppose you blame me for the things that happened to you, she said. Nothing happened to me, I told her. You were moved from place to place, you had no home of your own. You must blame me for that. I don't blame you for anything, I told her. You're a good boy, she said, stroking my face. You were always a good boy. Her fingers were rougher than I remembered them.

I stayed for an hour. I was happy to stay that long. And then I was happy to leave. You'll have to let me know how you get on with all those things you want to do, she said, trying to put a five-euro note into my hand, but I made a fist of it and kept it close against my side. I didn't want her money. I will, I said. I hope we can start again, she said. I hope so too, I told her, turning my phone on for it was evening now and the calls would start soon. Can I see you again sometime, she asked me. I could phone you and we could meet for lunch. You have my number, I told her.

It was raining as I walked home. When the phone rang

in my pocket, I thought it might be her but no, it was a man. Where do you live, I asked him. Smithfield. I'm only ten minutes from there, I said. Can you come over immediately, he asked me.

I can, I said.

The Country You Called Home

The brick crashed through the front window shortly after midnight and Émile woke with a start, his heart pounding, his eyes raw from interrupted sleep. The room was dark and as he reached across for the wristwatch that lay on the bedside table, he knocked it off and heard it land on the wooden floor with a heartbreaking crack.

'No!' he whispered to himself in dismay.

His father had given him the wristwatch two weeks earlier as a present for his ninth birthday and he treasured it. Looking down now, he saw that the glass that covered its face had shattered, scattering splinters across the floor. The watch wasn't new, of course. It had belonged to his grandfather, William Cross, who had bought it more than fifty years before on the morning he left Newcastle to begin a new life in West Cork. He'd passed it down to his son, Stephen, who in turn had given it to Émile, telling him that he needed to take great care of it for it was a precious family heirloom.

And now it was broken.

The boy put his head in his hands, wondering how he would ever tell his dad.

A moment later, he heard his parents' bedroom door open and the sound of their feet running along the hall-way into the front parlour of their small cottage and Émile remembered the noise that had woken him in the first place.

He jumped out of bed, his left foot landing on one of the small shards of glass, and sank to the floor, curling his foot around to examine the damage. A small chip, like a piece of broken ice, was half submerged in the ball of his foot and he turned his thumb and index finger into a pair of pincers to pull it out. A spot of blood appeared in its wake but he pressed his hand against it and when he took it away again it had disappeared. Standing up, he tested his weight on the injured foot before opening his bedroom door and following his parents into the parlour.

'Émile,' said Marie, turning around when she heard him. 'What are you doing up?'

His mother was wearing her nightdress and her hair hung down loosely around her shoulders. He hated seeing her like this. Marie usually wore her hair up in a tight bun and even though she didn't own many clothes she always made an effort to look elegant. Stephen, Émile's father, put it down to her French upbringing. He said women looked after themselves over there, not like Irish women who'd go around in a potato sack every day except Sunday if they could. But seeing her like this, in the middle of the night, she looked old and tired and not Marie-like at all.

'I heard a noise,' he said. 'It woke me up.'

'Don't come over here in your bare feet, son,' said

Stephen, who had taken yesterday's newspaper off the table and was using a brush to sweep the broken glass from the window on to the front page.

'The window!' said Émile, pointing across the room. A breeze was blowing through, making the net curtains on either side dance in the early-morning air like a pair of young girls waltzing in their nightclothes. 'What happened?'

'Someone put a brick through it,' said Stephen.

'But why?'

'Émile, step back,' said Marie, putting her hands on his shoulders and pulling him away from the fragments of glass. 'Just until your father is finished.'

'Why would someone put a brick through our window?' asked Émile, looking up at her.

'It was an accident,' said Stephen.

'How can a brick fly through a window by accident?'

'Émile, go back to bed,' said Marie, raising her voice now. 'Stephen, should I look outside to see if they're still there?'

'No, I'll do it.'

He folded the newspaper into a neat package, the broken glass wrapped carefully inside, and placed it on top of the table before reaching for the latch on the front door.

'Wait,' cried Marie, running into the kitchen and returning with the heavy copper saucepan that she used to make soup.

'What's this for?' asked Stephen, staring at it with a confused smile on his face, the kind of smile he always

41

wore when Marie did something that both baffled and amused him.

'To hit him with,' said Marie.

'To hit who with?'

'Whoever threw the brick.'

Émile looked around the floor and saw a rectangular shape lying beneath the table, brick-like for certain, but it was enclosed in paper and the whole parcel was held together by string, like a Christmas present. His mind raced with possibilities for who might have done such a thing. He was currently engaged in a war with Donal Higgins who lived two doors down and their acts of retaliation had grown over the last few days. But it was hard to imagine Donal doing something as bad as this and, anyway, he was probably in bed since he had to go to sleep at eight o'clock every night while Émile was allowed to stay up until half past.

'I don't think whoever it was will be waiting outside for me, do you?' asked Stephen, opening the front door while Marie stood behind him, holding the saucepan on high as he stepped out on to the street. Émile picked up the brick and began to untie the twine. It came loose easily enough and as the paper unfurled he was surprised to realize that he recognized it. He smoothed out the creases now, pressing it flat against the kitchen table, and examined it carefully. Green, white and orange, the colours of the Tricolour itself, the poster bore a picture of a serious-looking man sporting a big white moustache. The words 'Tyneside Irish Battalion' were written across the top with 'Irishmen – To Arms' inscribed beneath a harp in the centre of a shamrock. 'Join To-Day' was its closing demand.

'What's that?' asked Marie, coming back into the parlour, and Émile lifted the poster to show her, watching as his mother closed her eyes for a moment and sighed before shaking her head, as if she was both surprised and not surprised by what she saw. 'I knew something like this would happen,' she said. 'I said so, didn't I? But your father had to have his own way.'

'But why would someone wrap it around a brick?'

'Émile, your foot,' she cried, ignoring the poster now as she looked down at the floor where a small streak of blood had stained the woodwork. 'I told you to keep away from the glass.'

'There's no one outside,' said Stephen as he came back inside, closing the front door behind him and putting the latch on.

'I knew those posters would only bring trouble,' said Marie.

'I know, love, but—'

'Don't *love* me,' she snapped, a rare moment of anger, for most days Marie and Stephen seemed to do nothing but laugh together.

'How was I to know that they'd attack our house?'

'What did you think they'd do, throw a party for you?'

'I didn't hurt my foot in here,' said Émile, unable to meet his father's eye as he told them what had happened when he woke up. 'I'm sorry,' he said when he was finished. 'It was an accident.'

'Ah Émile,' said Stephen, coming over and lifting the

boy up to carry him back to bed. 'Don't be worrying about something like that. I can fix it. Sure I've broken the glass many times myself. Trust me, we have bigger things to worry about right now.'

Émile had heard the stories many times but he never grew tired of them.

The story of how his grandfather had left England when all his friends were signing up to fight the Boers in South Africa but he wanted no part of killing people whose name he couldn't even spell correctly. Instead, he came to the south coast of Ireland where he met an Irish girl, married her and brought up their son, Stephen, to love dogs, the ukulele and the novels of Sir Walter Scott.

The story of how Marie left France for Ireland when her parents died and Stephen found her sitting in a tea shop on the afternoon of her twenty-third birthday while he was strolling back to his father's farm.

The story of how he'd sat by the village pump until she came out and he asked her to come to a dance with him some night and she said, 'I don't go dancing with strange men,' and he said, 'Sure I'm not strange, do I seem strange to you, I'm not a bit strange, am I?'

The story of how the dance had gone well, not to mention the wedding at Clonakilty parish church later that same year and how they'd wanted a child for a long time but none would come and only when they'd given up on the idea of it did Émile suddenly appear, out of the blue, a gift to the pair of them, and then their family was complete and neither of them had ever been so happy in all their lives as when there was just the three of them together at home, cuddled up on the sofa, reading their books.

These were stories that Émile had heard many, many times. But sure how could he ever grow tired of hearing them when they made him feel so wanted, so happy and so loved?

The posters had arrived four days before the night of the broken window in a long tube sealed in cardboard and brown tape, with eight stamps on the surface bearing the image of King George, who looked like an awful grump. Mr Devlin, the local postman, waited until evening time to deliver it. Émile suspected that he'd been watching out for Stephen to return home from work and only then did he knock on the door.

'What do you suppose it is?' asked Stephen as he, Marie, Mr Devlin and Émile stood at all four corners of the kitchen table, staring at the tube as if it was an unexploded bomb.

'There's only one way to find out,' said Mr Devlin. 'Would you not open it, Stephen, no?'

'Ah I don't know about that,' said Stephen, shaking his head and frowning. 'Sure you'd never know what might be in there.'

'Oh for pity's sake,' said Marie, taking the bread knife from the counter and picking up the tube to slice her way down the tape. 'We can't just stare at it all night.'

'Be careful there, Mrs,' said Mr Devlin, standing back as if he was afraid that it might blow up in all their faces.

'Will Mrs Devlin not have your tea on?' she replied, taking the cap off the tube and giving it a shake until the rolled-up sheets of paper eased their way out into her hand. 'Should you not be getting home?'

'The food is always burnt to a crisp as it is. A few extra minutes won't make it any less edible.'

Marie sighed as she held the posters out for everyone to see.

'What's this now?' asked Mr Devlin, leaning forward and reading them for himself. 'This has something to do with the war, is it?'

Stephen picked up the tube and shook it again and a note fell out. His eyes moved back and forth across the lines, his lips mouthing the words quietly to himself.

'Goodnight, Mr Devlin,' he said a moment later, turning to the postman.

'There was something else in there, was there?' he asked, pointing at the note. 'Is it an explanation of some sort?'

'Goodnight, Mr Devlin,' repeated Stephen, opening the front door and standing there with his hand on the latch until the postman gave in and made his way towards it.

'There was a time when a man got a cup of tea when he visited a house,' he announced in an insulted tone as he left. 'Those days are gone now, it seems. Goodnight all!'

'What's in the note?' asked Émile, when there was just the three of them left.

'Maybe you should go to your room,' said Stephen.

'Who is it from?' asked Marie.

'James.'

'James who?'

'James, my cousin James.'

'In Newcastle?'

'Yes.'

'And what does he say?'

Stephen cleared his throat and began to read.

Dear Stephen, he said.

*I'm sorry I haven't written in so long but I'm not a man
for letters, as you know. All is well here but it's raining
today. Here are posters that you can paste around your
town as we need as many ~~soliders~~ soldiers as we can find
or we're going to lose this war. I know all you Irish don't
know which side to stand on but you'll be better off on
ours. We'll see you right for it in the end, I'm sure of that.*

*I have bad news. Do you remember the Williams
twins who you used to pal around with when your dad
brought you over to see us when you were a lad? Both
killed at Verdun. And Georgie Summerfield, who lived
next door to us? Well he's been in hospital these last few
months, they say he can't stop shaking or hold a sensible
conversation. It's a rotten business but –*

He stopped reading and put the letter down.

'Oh,' said Marie, her forehead wrinkling a little as she
thought about this.

Émile wondered why Georgie Summerfield couldn't
stop shaking but guessed it had something to do with
the war. It had been going on for almost three years now,
since July 1914. His parents and his teachers never grew

47

tired of talking about it even though it was happening across the sea in Europe, which was *miles* away from West Cork. A boy he knew, Séamus Kilduff, had an older brother who'd signed up to fight with the Brits and half the town said he was a traitor for taking sides with a bunch of Sassenachs who'd been making life hell for the Irish for years. The other half said he was very brave to put himself in danger for people he didn't even know and that the only way to secure peace was for everyone who believed in the freedom of nations to do their bit. There was fierce debate over it and everyone took a side. Émile heard stories about fights in the local pub and a rule being made on the GAA team that no one could discuss Séamus Kilduff's brother before a match as it only led to trouble. But then word came that he'd been killed in the Battle of the Somme and the whole town turned out for his funeral. Father Macallie said he was a credit to his family, a credit to his religion and above all a credit to West Cork, which would one day achieve independence from the rest of Ireland and be allowed to manage its own affairs as God intended.

A copy of the *Skibbereen Eagle* appeared in their cottage most evenings and Marie pored over it, engrossed by every piece of information that she could find. Her own country, after all, was being overwhelmed by fighting. Her two brothers had fought to keep the Germans out of their home town of Reims but both had been arrested and she hadn't heard from them in a long time. Émile had learned not to mention their names, as she would only start crying inconsolably.

But Marie wasn't the only one who read the papers. Émile did too. He'd become interested the previous Easter, when all the trouble had been happening up in Dublin and a group of men had barricaded themselves into the General Post Office on O'Connell Street demanding that the Irish be left alone to look after Ireland and the English had come along and said, *sorry about that, lads, but no chance.* And there'd been lots of shooting and lots of killing and one of the men from the GPO had been brought out in a terrible sickness, barely knowing who he was or what he was doing, and was tied to a chair so the English could turn their guns on him for showing cheek to their King.

'Why would they fight for the English?' he asked now, looking down at the letter on the table.

'They?' asked Stephen, turning his head quickly and staring at his son; it wasn't often that he had a flash of anger like this. 'Who's this *they* that you're talking about, son?'

'The Irish,' said Émile quietly.

'The Irish are a *they* now, are they?' he asked.

'Stephen, stop it,' said Marie.

'Stop what?'

'Just stop it.'

'Come on ahead,' said Stephen irritably, shaking his head. 'I'll not be having *they*s in this house.'

Émile looked from his father to his mother and back again, angry and upset at being spoken to like this. 'Well I don't know, do I?' he cried, trying to hold back tears. 'You're English, Mum's French, sometimes you tell me I'm

49

Irish, other times you tell me I'm half English and half French.'

'You're Irish,' said Stephen. 'And don't you forget it.'

But he wasn't fully Irish, he knew that. The boys at school picked on him and said he was only a blow-in and that if your family hadn't lived in Ireland since before Cromwell had started his slaughter of the innocents then you had no business being here anyway. And why did he have to be anything, he wondered? The Irish hated the English, the English hated the Germans, the Germans hated the French, so it seemed that if you lived in a country, you had to have someone to hate. But then Cork people hated the Kerry people, and the Kerry people hated the Dubliners, and the Dubs were split in two by the Liffey, with the families who lived in the tenements in the city centre hated by all. It seemed to Émile that you weren't allowed to be alive unless you had someone to hate and someone to hate you in return.

'You're right,' said Stephen, reaching forward and pulling Émile's head into his shoulder for a moment. 'I'm sorry, son. I shouldn't have snapped.'

Marie stood up, gathering up the posters and taking them over towards the fireplace.

'What are you doing?' asked Stephen, staring at her.

'The sensible thing,' she said, peeling one off, folding it in half and then half again, before reaching its corner into the flames and letting the fire take a catch of it before she allowed it to sink into the hearth and burn. Then she unpeeled the second one and started to fold it too but Stephen was too quick for her; he was on his feet in a jiffy, pulling the posters out of her arms.

'Stop that now,' he shouted.

'Why?'

'They're not for burning.'

Émile reached over for the letter, wanting to know what else it said, but Marie pulled it out of his hands and put it on the top shelf of the dresser, next to the key for the outside lav.

'Did no one ever tell you not to read other people's letters?' she asked, staring down at her son. Émile said nothing in reply but looked at his father instead.

'What does James want you to do with those posters?' he asked.

'Paste them up around the town. See if any of the men here will sign up.'

'Do you think they will?'

Stephen shook his head. 'Probably not,' he said.

'Then there's no point doing it,' said Marie.

'Oh, I'll do it all right.'

'Why?'

'Because it's the right thing.'

'The right thing for who?'

Stephen shrugged his shoulders. 'If the Germans win,' he said, 'if they conquer England, where do you think they'll go next? Have a think about it, love. What's the next country along?'

Marie threw her arms in the air. 'If you put those posters up around here,' she said, 'our neighbours will call you a traitor. Like they did with Séamus Kilduff's brother.'

'Who everyone said was a hero in the end.'

'They said he was a hero when they were putting him in the ground. They didn't say anything like that when he was walking above it.'

'You're not going away to fight, are you, Dad?' asked Émile, his eyes opening wide in horror at the idea.

'I don't know, son,' replied Stephen. 'But it's something that I've been thinking about. After all, the sooner the war is over, the sooner we can all live in peace.'

'No!' shouted Émile, jumping up. 'No, you can't. Mum, tell him he can't.'

'Stephen, you're upsetting the boy. And throw those things away before they land us all in trouble.'

'It's only a few posters. Those who want to take an interest can and those who don't, well they don't have to.'

'Don't be so naive,' snapped Marie as Émile rushed to her side and pressed himself against her. 'You have no idea what will happen to you if you put them up around town. To us. To all of us. *Irishmen – To Arms,*' she added, laughing bitterly. 'They want us on their side when they need help, that's for sure. But when they don't—'

'Us! Them! You! Me!' shouted Stephen. 'If you ask me, we all choose our pronouns depending on what suits us at the time!'

And that was the end of that. Marie stormed off to her bedroom, Stephen stayed in the front parlour for a smoke, and Émile grabbed the key for the outside lav and ran down in the cold night air. He'd been desperate for a pee ever since Mr Devlin had arrived with the post but he couldn't leave the front parlour when there was so much going on.

Émile went with his father when he placed the posters in prominent positions around town, and when the townspeople saw them, there was an outcry. A meeting was held in the church and Émile listened as Stephen made the case that here was something bigger than the argument between England and Ireland – that, he said, could be returned to at a later date and hopefully with wiser, more peaceful heads, but in the meantime there was a bigger fight being played out across Europe – and the Irish couldn't stick their heads under their blankets forever because sooner or later it would come their way. 'We've spent centuries trying to win the land back for ourselves,' he told them. 'And we're this close. You can feel it. I can feel it. We're on the cusp, lads. Now tell me, all of you, what if we win our country back and lose it all over again to someone else? Where's the victory in that?'

Donal Higgins' father had fought the opposite case. 'The enemy of my enemy is my friend,' he said. 'Did you never hear that line, no? Why on earth would we spend all this time trying to get the English out of Ireland only to help them in their hour of need? Could someone please explain that to me, for it makes no sense as far as I can see!'

'But look, if we help out now, maybe that'll be the difference between victory and defeat,' argued Stephen.

'Let them be defeated!' cried Donal Higgins' father.

'And then what? If this war doesn't end soon and with

fairness on all sides, you can mark my words that there will be another along before too long and you'll be too old to fight in it and I'll be too old to fight in it but our sons won't! Your Donal will be of an age. And my Émile. So think on before you say we should just ignore what's going on.'

There was an almighty debate and Émile couldn't hear any of the arguments any more as voices were raised so high, and finally Father Macallie had to take to the altar and call the meeting to an end, for it was clear that there was never going to be agreement between the sides and if it didn't stop there'd be a fistfight in the church.

Émile sat at the back and tried to reason it through in his mind. He could see both sides of this. But brave young soldiers who were fighting on the Continent to make sure that everyone got to live as they wanted to live – it seemed to him that this was the side worth fighting for.

When he thought about it for too long, however, it made his head hurt, that was the truth of it.

But the posters went up, and Stephen's part in it – that couldn't be denied. And a few nights later, the brick came flying through the front window, waking up the house and causing Émile to reach out so quickly that his grandfather's watch smashed on the floor.

Six weeks later, when Émile found out that Stephen had signed up to fight for the British Expeditionary Force, he felt frightened and proud at the same time. But he knew that the whole town was in a quandary over it because everyone liked Stephen. He'd grown up among them, after all. He'd married a woman they all respected, had a son who was a fine fellow altogether and had never done a moment's harm to anyone in all his life. Yes, the English were the enemy, but at least they all knew who the English were. If the Germans won, then it was anyone's guess what might happen to Ireland next.

Émile ended up in another fight with Donal Higgins, whose father said that Stephen was a turncoat and a blaggard for falling in with a bunch of Sassenach ne'er-do-wells and if he was any sort of Irishman then he'd never fight for a country that had done all they could to keep the Irish in servitude for eight hundred years.

'Your dad's a traitor,' said Donal Higgins, keeping his left arm close to his waist and his fist clenched as his right jabbed out and made contact with Émile's chin.

'And your dad's a coward,' said Émile, punching low to Donal's waist with his right hand while his left gave him an almighty clatter around the head.

'You'll take that back,' said Donal, kicking out.

'I'll do no such thing,' said Émile, launching himself forward and throwing himself on top of Donal, his whole body lashing out in the hope that he'd hit something important and the fight would come to an end as quickly as possible.

It took two teachers to separate them and they were both put in the bad books for fighting.

They all came out to see him off the morning that he left for the war and those who were old enough remembered the day, over twenty years before, when they'd done the same thing for his father. The arguments about the Irish taking part hadn't changed during that time but no one wanted to see any harm come to one of the town's favourite sons.

He woke early, just after five o'clock, ready to join a small group of young men who were taking a bus together to Rosslare and then a boat across to Plymouth and a train to the centre of England where they were to be taken to a camp to begin basic training. Lying in bed, his eyes on the ceiling, he wondered whether he would survive whatever was to follow and whether he would ever see West Cork again. Whether he would ever hold his wife in his arms or take a hurley out to the fields with his son as he'd done every Saturday morning for the last few years. And finally, the minutes passed and what choice did he have but to get out of bed, have a wash, dress in the uniform they'd given him and get himself ready to say his goodbyes.

They gathered on the street, his wife crying for fear of what might happen to him, his nine-year-old son standing in the corner of the doorway, trying his best to be a brave man even though every part of him knew that he might never see his father again.

'I'll write when I get there,' said Émile.

'Make sure you do,' she said.

'You're the man of the house now,' he said, turning to the boy. 'You look after your mother while I'm gone, do you hear me, Stephen?'

'I will, Dad,' said Stephen, standing up tall, determined not to cry while the whole street was watching him.

'Now take this,' said Émile, reaching into his pocket and handing across his grandfather's watch, whose glass had been broken and mended half a dozen times over the years but still told the time without fail. 'It's a family heirloom. And you look after it for me until I get home, all right? Because I'm coming back here for that watch and for you.'

They drove across to Rosslare in silence for the most part. Donal Higgins told a few jokes and the others tried to join in but the truth was they were too afraid of what was to come to join in the laughter. Émile sat, staring out the window, thinking of his father and all that he'd suffered during the last war, the one they called *the Great War*. He'd put up those posters, he'd tried to recruit people to fight for what was right and the people of the town had turned on him, but he had fought on regardless and finally taken four of the lads from the town with him to the trenches where all but one of them had fallen, all but one of them had given their lives for peace, all but one of them were buried in a cemetery where their families could only visit once or twice in their lives, for wasn't the price of the boat across to the Continent only shocking?

Stephen hadn't been the one to come home. He'd died just short of a year after arriving in France. He'd written home every week while he was there and he'd kept his spirits up and stayed good-hearted and he'd been sure that whatever the differences were between England and Ireland, this war was something bigger than all of that and every good man needed to play his part for peace.

And now it was his son's turn.

Émile met his sergeant, he trained, he collapsed in exhaustion and then got up again. He felt his body grow thick with muscle, he thought he could give nothing more, he had no more to give, and then he gave some more. He collapsed under the pain of it, he fought out the other side of it. He realized that he was made of strong stuff, that he was his father's son. He reached the end, he passed out, he was applauded, he took another train to Southampton where he boarded a boat for France and the uncertainty that lay ahead.

He lay in his bunk the night before the first battle began and thought of that night when he was just a boy and a brick had come through the parlour window and life as he knew it began to change.

'What's your name?' asked the boy in the bed next to his.

'Émile,' said Émile.

'You're French?'

'My mother is. My father was English. He died in the Great War.'

'And you?'

Émile hesitated. It still came down to this end, didn't it? Who you were, where you came from, how you defined yourself. The country you called home.

'I'm Irish,' he said, before rolling over and trying to find some sleep.

The Schleinermetzenmann

I never had a chance to observe Arthur in his public role until a few days before my mother's funeral. We grew up next door to each other, the closest of friends throughout our younger years, but drifted apart in adulthood for all the usual reasons. Almost a decade earlier, with my nascent and much-longed-for career already smothered in its cradle like a mewling infant, I decided to spend a summer travelling and somehow lost track of time, building a new life far away from anyone who knew me. Arthur, in fact, came to the airport to see me off and just as I was about to make my way through the security gates he asked whether I would mind if he called Becky, a girl I had briefly been dating earlier that year, and invited her out for a drink. 'She has amazing tits,' he told me, which was true, although I had got no closer to seeing them in their exposed state than he had for she subscribed to some outdated and frankly nonsensical ideas regarding maintaining her virginity until her wedding night.

'Do whatever you like,' I told him, thinking this was a disappointing way for him to say goodbye to his oldest friend. 'I don't care.'

We seemed to lose track of each other after that and when I eventually dug out his email address and wrote to tell him that my mother had died, he wrote back almost immediately, offering condolences while inviting me to a reading he was giving at a city-centre bookshop the following day, to be followed, he said, by an evening of alcohol-fuelled reminiscing.

I had no great desire to see him in front of an audience but nevertheless I went along and was surprised to see that he'd become a little bit famous, or as famous as a novelist can get anyway, for a sizeable crowd had gathered to hear him tell us all how wonderful he was.

'Before writing this novel,' he said, putting both hands to his face and dragging them slowly across the skin, as if his fingers might offer an early-evening exfoliant, 'I had a serious case of what our German friends call . . .' He paused for a moment and looked around the room. 'Are there any Germans here?' he asked, and if there were, no one spoke up. 'Good,' he said. 'I had a serious case of what our German friends call *kästellfrügenschänge*, which literally means the sensation a man feels when he is standing on a precipice, usually but not necessarily naked, preparing to jump to his death but being held back by a feeling that he might yet be of some use to the world.' He smiled gently and shook his head as if he could not quite believe that he had ever doubted his own genius. 'But when the words came?' He wagged his finger at us as if we were unruly children. 'No more *kästellfrügenschänge*.'

The audience, morons all, lapped it up. I could see two

university-aged girls, pretty if you like that sort of thing, doing everything they could to make eye contact with him. And I'm sure the boy next to me emitted a faintly erotic sigh at my old friend's supposed bilingualism. For my part, I found it hard not to laugh out loud, for I had spent most of the last few years living in a town called Tittmoning on the German-Austrian border and had become fluent in the language. (I work on a large dairy farm where, in fact, I have my own brand of local celebrity as the *kuhliebhabermann* – which literally means a man who has a suspiciously close emotional relationship to cattle – a nickname I acquired for no other reason than the fact that I try to treat all my cows, especially the good-looking ones, with atypical kindness before sending them off to the slaughterhouse in Burghausen to be stunned by electrical currents and have their throats slit.) And I can promise you that *kästellfrügenschänge* is not a real word. It's just a jumble of sounds placed next to each other that have a faintly Germanic ring to them.

My sighing neighbour, trembling before greatness, raised his hand.

'A question,' said Arthur, pointing towards the boy, whose face immediately turned fire-engine red.

'Please, sir,' he whispered, like an older, ganglier, gayer version of Oliver Twist. 'Please, sir, what advice would you give to young writers?'

Arthur tapped his upper lip with his index finger as he considered this. I rolled my eyes; this could hardly be the first time he'd been asked such an obvious question. Surely he had a stock answer tucked away somewhere.

'Have you ever visited the southern of the two Brelitzen Islands?' he said finally, after much thought.

'No,' said the boy, shaking his head.

'The northern one perhaps?'

'No.'

'What about the Cassandra Strait, that spiteful stimulant of cerulean that separates the two?'

'I've never been anywhere,' said the boy, becoming noticeably aroused now by such close attention. 'Except to EuroDisney once with my uncle Mark when I was twelve.'

'The Brelitzen Islands,' said Arthur, smiling. 'Go to the Brelitzen Islands. You'll know why when you get there.'

I felt myself beginning to grow angry. I'm not an expert on world geography by any means but I had never heard of the Brelitzen Islands and doubted their existence. Still, I said nothing. God forbid that I should piss all over the magic.

'Creating art,' declared Arthur a moment later, apropos of nothing, while holding his wretched novel in the air, 'reminds me of why I look forward to death so much. At the heart of our mortality lies what the Shīn-du monks on Mount Hejiji call *shrān-kao*.' He shook his head. 'No,' he said, 'I'm pronouncing that wrong, amn't I? It's *shrān-kaoj*, I think. With a silent "j" at the end?'

He looked around but no one said anything. They were staring at him like he was the love child of the Dalai Lama and Oprah Winfrey. An old lady, close to tears at such life-changing wisdom, blew her nose loudly, sounding like a steam engine about to depart a platform in *The Railway Children*.

'Yes, I think that's it. *Shrān-kaoj*. Forgive me, Gampopo!'

Both pronunciations had sounded exactly the same to me and they were, I'm sure, equally meaningless. I also doubted the existence of Shīn-du monks or of Mount Hejiji itself, which, for what it's worth, he pronounced *He-ki-ki*.

'But life,' he added, banging his index finger sharply against the dust jacket, which showed a young boy walking with his back to the reader along a road towards a moonlit horizon. 'Life is art and art is pain and pain is what makes us know that we are alive.' He held the book aloft now and waved it at us with all the zeal of John Knox brandishing the Book of Common Prayer in the face of Mary, Queen of Scots. 'And I am alive,' he roared then, a blue vein beginning to assert its presence on his forehead. 'I'm alive!'

Really, considering that we were only meeting again because I was preparing to bury my mother, I thought the whole performance was a little over the top.

Later, in the pub, Arthur told me that he didn't want to know anything about what had happened to me during my years abroad. He asked me not to speak about the friends I had made, the experiences that had changed me or any love affairs that I might have enjoyed. He didn't even want to hear about my cows and I have many interesting stories to tell about them if people are only prepared to listen.

'As an artist,' he explained, 'as a creative person, I prefer to rely on my imagination. I have memories of the boy you once were, Mulligan, and ideas about the man you might have become. Let's not spoil the narrative by drizzling reality over it.'

'Why do you keep calling me by my surname?' I asked. 'Why don't you call me Pierce?'

'I've always hated that name,' said Arthur. 'Even when we were children, foraging for adventure like truffling pigs in the woods, comparing penis sizes in darkened glades—'

'That never happened,' I said.

'Even then I didn't like the name Pierce,' he continued, ignoring me. 'There's something so unbearably common about it. No, I think Mulligan is a far better name. You don't meet many Mulligans any more.'

'Well, I don't want you calling me that,' I said.

'Fine, then I shall call you Darling.'

'No, that won't work either.'

'It's either Mulligan or Darling, darling. You decide. Now would you mind if I swapped seats with you? I prefer to keep my back to the room.'

'Why?' I asked, standing up and moving around to his side of the table.

'The punters, darling,' he said. 'Everyone is trying not to look at me but in doing so they're making me feel very self-conscious. If I have my back to them, perhaps they'll stop not-staring.'

'I really don't think anyone recognizes you,' I said, looking around at the bar, which was defined by its over-whelming indifference to our presence. Three young men, likely strangers to literature, were watching a football match on the television, their tabletop littered with glasses and empty crisp packets. A few old men were seated silently at the bar, contemplating the ruins of their lives. A woman was typing on a MacBook Air while drinking gin after gin after gin.

'You have no idea what it's like to be watched all the time, darling,' said Arthur. 'It's a wonder I'm not a recluse in some luxury hotel suite.'

'Can you stop calling me darling, please?'

'Of course, Mulligan. You see, one doesn't write for fame or glory but sometimes that's what happens. Consider a packhorse wandering into an untilled field and . . .' He stopped and reconsidered the beginnings of his analogy before shaking his head. 'No, forget that,' he said. 'It won't work. By the way, did you read what Robertson wrote about Clive?'

'Yes,' I said. (Naturally, I hadn't; nor did I have any idea who either Robertson or Clive were. Nor did I care.) 'Let's not talk about it. Look, the reason I came to your reading—'

'Did you enjoy it?'

'It was fine.'

'Just fine?'

'It was very good.'

'What was wrong with it?'

'Nothing was wrong with it. The audience seemed to enjoy it.'

'You were part of the audience.'

'Well yes,' I admitted. 'In a manner of speaking.'

'You were sitting among them.'

'But you invited me.'

'And you came.'

'Because I needed to see you.'

'The woman behind me. With the MacBook Air,' he said, leaning forward. 'If she comes over, tell her that we're old friends who haven't seen each other in a long time and—'

'Well, that's actually true,' I pointed out.

'She's probably writing a book,' he said. 'She'll ask me to read it. There's no way that I will but I don't want to disappoint her.'

'I don't think she's even aware of us,' I said.

'Perhaps she's shy.' He turned and looked at her, flashing a set of very white teeth. 'I don't bite,' he shouted, causing every head in the place to turn in his direction. 'My prose does, yes. But I do not.'

He turned back to me with a shrug, as if to say that it was no easy thing being as brilliant as him.

'Did you read my novel?' he asked me.

'I did,' I said.

'And what did you think of it?'

'I thought the reviews were a little cruel, to be honest. I didn't think it was as bad as they made out.'

His face darkened a little and he took a long drink from his pint. 'I never read reviews,' he said.

'Then why do all the good ones show up on your Facebook page?'

'I couldn't tell you,' he said. 'Someone is probably hacking my account.'

'Does it hurt?' I asked.

'Does what hurt? Being hacked? I imagine my phone is being hacked, you know. Bloody tabloids. They hate all of us' – he made inverted comma symbols in the air – '"celebrities".'

'Bad reviews,' I said. 'Do you find them depressing?'

'It's better than getting no reviews, I suppose.'

I felt a stab of pain in my chest; that was unkind of him.

'Most reviews are written out of professional jealousy,' he continued, apparently oblivious to my discomfort. 'The so-called journalists who write them know that I'm the best thing in this town and they hate me for it. The only reviews I read are the ones published in the French papers. They value literature in France. Not like here. But look, darling Mulligan, it is good to see you again after all these years. We've gotten older, haven't we? You've changed so much. I don't think I would have known you if you'd walked past me on the street. You used to have such a boyish complexion.'

'When I was a boy, I suppose,' I agreed. 'And I'm glad you've decided to accept what happened with your hair. The shaved look suits you. I'd shave this mop off if I could. It takes so much upkeep.'

'But it helps to cover up the wrinkles on your forehead,' he said. 'And your acne cleared up too, I see. God, you were just plagued by that as a teenager, weren't you? Remember how you could never get a girlfriend?'

I nodded – this was a painful memory – and glanced at my watch.

'Do you have someplace to be?' he asked.

'No, I was just checking the time.'

'What time is it? I never wear a watch. I can't bear to feel trapped by an artificial conceit.'

'I'm not sure time is an artificial conceit,' I said. 'The sun goes round the earth, the day grows steadily brighter, then darker. It's not complicated. And it's almost nine o'clock.'

'The sun doesn't go round the earth, darling,' he said. 'Strike that, reverse it, as Mr Wonka said. But I'm sure you just misspoke. Anyway, look, I haven't said how sorry I was to hear of your mother's death.' He reached across and took both my hands in his. For a moment I thought he was going to kiss them. 'I'm so very, very sorry,' he said, looking me directly in the eyes.

'Thank you.'

'Natural causes, was it?'

'Yes, thankfully. She died in her sleep.'

'Not murdered then?'

I stared at him, uncertain that I had heard him correctly.

'No,' I said, shaking my head. 'Why on earth would she have been murdered?'

'No reason. But there are so many disturbed individuals abroad these days. I'm always nervous of some *Catcher in the Rye*-wielding maniac approaching me in a dark alley late at night and wanting to connect his narrative to mine in some homicidal way. I have no desire to be a martyr to art. When I think of what happened to John . . .' He shook his head, pained to the core.

'John who?'

'John Lennon.'

'You call him John?' I asked. 'Were you friends? Weren't you nine when he died?'

'There's a connection, you know? It's hard to explain to someone who isn't an artist. Any more.'

'Thanks,' I said.

'Trust me,' he replied. 'You're better off out of it.'

'Am I? That's good to know.'

'Anyway, I'm sure it won't come to that. The chances of me being murdered are slim.'

'Oh I don't know about that.'

'Really?' He looked up, apparently pleased by the idea.

'Anyway,' I said. 'The evening my mother died, we opened her will.'

'Was there a codicil?' he asked. 'I've always loved the word *codicil*. Someday I plan to write a novel called *The Codicil of Agnès Fontaine*. I have no idea what it will be about but it's a magnificent title, don't you think? Promise me you won't breathe a word of it to anyone.'

'I promise,' I said. 'I've already forgotten it.'

'Thank you, darling. So am I to assume that your mother left me something?'

'No. Why would she do that?'

'It seemed like a natural deduction from the way the conversation was going, that's all. And you must remember, your mother and I were very close when I was a child. I stayed in touch with her all those years while you were off inter-railing around Europe or whatever it is that you were doing. In many ways, she was more of a mother to me than my father ever was.'

This was not as bizarre a statement as it might sound. Arthur's mother died when he was a baby and in her absence his father had been left to play both parental roles. A hugely accomplished transvestite, very popular within both the club scene and the more progressive elements of the media, Arthur's father switched between genders every seven days, being a father to his son one week and a mother to him the next. He was a strong believer that a child needed both parents. And he was a magnificent father, as far I recall, taking him to soccer matches and letting him stay up late on school nights, but really an atrocious mother. She suffocated him.

'That's nice of you to say, Arthur,' I said. 'I know she was very fond of you.'

'Don't you hate the way *fond* as a synonym for *foolish* has become arcane?' he asked me.

'I didn't know that it ever was.'

'Oh yes. You find it throughout Elizabethan and Jacobean literature. Ben, Kit, Will, John – they all used it. Anyway, I'm not surprised. I suppose I was like the son she never had.'

'Well, she had me.'

'I visited her book club once, did she tell you that?'

'No.'

'Such elegant ladies. Powdered and perfumed. All of a certain age, of course, but still bristling with sexuality. I had offers, you know.'

'I'd rather not hear about them, thanks.'

A roar went up from the football table and then there was much placing of heads in hands while one sole traitor to their cause – wearing different colours to his comrades, I noticed – stood up and pointed at the screen, shouting 'Get in!' over and over at the top of his voice.

'In her will, she asked that you say a few words over her grave. Nothing too . . . elaborate, mind you. Or lengthy.'

'Did she specify that?'

'No, that was me. But I think it's what she meant.'

'I would be honoured,' he said, bowing his head slowly. 'When does the dreadful event take place?'

'Tuesday morning.'

He finished off the rest of his drink and nodded. 'Email me the details and I'll be there. Until then, mon semblable, mon frère, I bid you adieu.' And with that, he was gone, sweeping through the door, his black cloak flaring out behind him like Dracula off on a night-hunt.

'Tosser,' I muttered under my breath.

Naturally, my sister was appalled at the idea of Arthur even attending the funeral, let alone speaking at it. 'I heard him on the radio a couple of weeks ago,' she told me, 'saying how he'd spent years trying *not* to write because he knew how painful it would be. And I don't think he meant for readers. I'd never heard such nonsense.'

'Have you read his novel?' I asked.

'Yes,' she said.

'And what did you think?'

'Oh, it's terrible,' she said. 'Absolutely ghastly. So wildly overwritten that it's almost a parody of itself. It never simply rains; the clouds dissolve in the glaucous firmament, weeping their lachrymosity upon the heads of the aberrant populace. No one is ever happy, instead they feel a warmth building inside their coccyx and rising through their alimentary canal as a sensation of well-being extends its octopus-like tentacles through the capillaries producing a sensation close to orgasm.'

'Thank you, Audrey,' I said. 'I'd rather not hear you use that word.'

'Does the idea of my having orgasms frighten you, Pierce?'

'It does if I'm in the room. Now can we move on, please? There's nothing to be done. I've asked Arthur, and more importantly Mother asked Arthur, so we should do what she wanted.'

'Can we give him a time limit at least?'

'I've told him to keep it short.' I took a sip from my coffee and recalled something, a bad memory rising from the mausoleum. 'Didn't you take Arthur to your Debs?' I asked after a moment. 'This person you so despise. Didn't you go out with each other for a while?'

'We did not go out with each other,' she said, turning on me. 'We did nothing of the sort. Yes, I invited him to my Debs but only because Steven Slipton broke his leg the previous week and couldn't come.'

'Slipton,' I said, recalling a tall, rather handsome young man who looked a little like Richard Harris in his prime. 'I always thought that was a funny name.'

'Ironically, he broke his leg after he—'

'Slipped somewhere, yes. I guessed. Still, you asked Arthur. Of the other two million or so penis-enabled humans in Ireland, you went after him.'

'I'm not proud of it,' she admitted, sitting down and offering the closest thing to a smile I had seen since she'd discovered Mother dead in her bed, a copy of *Fifty Shades of Grey* clutched in her stiffening hands. She would never discover how it turned out now.

'You loved him,' I said. 'You loved Arthur. You wanted to undress him and do dirty things with his naked body.'

'Actually, I did,' she said. 'After the Debs. Out the back of the Burlington car park.'

'Oh Christ,' I said, putting my cup down. 'I was kidding. You don't mean that you actually had sex with him?'

'Of course I had sex with him,' she said. 'It was my Debs. It would have been rude not to. And you can say whatever you like, you and he were inseparable when you were children.'

'That was a long time ago. Before he became an insufferable ass.'

'He told me that you used to compare penis sizes.'

'What is his obsession with that? That never happened.'

'He told me he won too.'

I rolled my eyes.

'Which,' she added, 'speaking from first-hand experience does not say very much about you.'

'I'll have you know that there's a certain milkmaid in Tittmoning who could contest that opinion. She's told me many times that I have nothing to worry about, that I'm perfectly average.'

'Well lucky her. And if you don't want to hear about

my orgasms, I don't want to hear about your perfectly average penis.'

'You brought it up,' I pointed out.

'Did I? You pervert, Pierce. I'm your sister.'

'That's not what I meant and you know it.'

'Nothing can happen between us, you realize that, don't you? We'd have three-headed children.'

'Oh shut up.'

She sniggered and looked out the window where her dog, Frisky, was living up to his name by attempting to mate with a bougainvillea. Perhaps aware that he was being watched, he stopped his rutting momentarily, hung his head in a this-is-what-I'm-reduced-to-since-you-won't-get-me-a-bitch-of-my-own way, and got back to it. He looked like he was having fun, at least.

'If he says anything inappropriate or just keeps banging on with no end in sight, then I'll tell him to stop,' said Audrey.

'Is that what you did on your Debs night?'

'I'm serious, Pierce. Why did Mother want him to talk anyway? What on earth was going through her mind?'

I shrugged. 'Who knows?' I said. 'She could be rather sentimental at times.'

'Not in her choice of reading material, she couldn't. Maybe she liked the idea of a celebrity appearing as she was lowered down.'

'A celebrity?' I laughed, outraged by such liberties being taken with the English language. 'You're kidding, right? Arthur's not a celebrity. He's just a writer. And he's only got one book to his name so far.'

'Well, that's how he likes to think of himself, isn't it? And perhaps Mother felt the same way. He has received a lot of attention for his work, you know.'

'Stalin received a lot of attention for his work too. It didn't make it any good.'

Leaving the kitchen, I wandered upstairs into Mother's room, where the windows had been flung open to release the smell of stale, dead woman. Someone had covered a mirror with a black negligee. I hadn't been in this room very much since I was a teenager and it still felt a little out of bounds to me, but as I looked around at the picture of the Sacred Heart on the wall, the plastic holy water vessel shaped like Jesus on the cross and the collection of erotic fiction on the bookshelves, I felt like I was being transported back to childhood, when Arthur and I would rummage around in here looking for Christmas presents. We'd do the same thing in his house, taking out his father's dresses and prancing around in front of the mirror like a couple of cheerful young benders until he caught us and chased us out.

And here on the dresser was a photograph of Mother with Father, both staring straight at the camera with no smiles on their faces, like a couple from a nineteenth-century portrait, all gloomy-eyed and horror-struck. And here a photo of Mother with Audrey and me. And here, to my surprise, one of her and Arthur at Butlin's. When on earth had they gone to Butlin's together? She'd never taken me to Butlin's.

*

At the graveyard, before starting his eulogy, Arthur requested that all cell phones be turned to silent or switched off and under no circumstances should photographs be taken. Also, he insisted that whatever he said in the next ten minutes – my heart sank at those words – should be forgotten by everyone after the burial and not reproduced by any means, including but not specifically limited to print or digital formats.

He was incorrect with his timings. In the end, he spoke for almost twenty minutes, by which time I imagine even my mother, decomposing in her ligneous sarcophagus (as Arthur himself might say), was probably growing restless. The priest, a pasty-faced fellow supporting himself on a crutch, was becoming visibly unstable, while several grieving friends and relatives were checking their watches, hoping that this would come to an end soon and we would be allowed to go to the pub.

Convinced by some veiled threats that Arthur made later in the day concerning lawsuits against those who infringed the copyright on his eulogy, I will refrain from reproducing his words, other than to say that they were what you might expect from a preening narcissist. There were an extraordinary number of mentions of how close he and my mother had once been, how he had come to see her in the nursing home before she died, where they had talked of Flaubert – fact: my mother was never in a nursing home and certainly never read a book in translation in her life, unless you count *Fifty Shades of Grey*, which was certainly not originally written in English – and how his life seemed a little more hollow, empty and vacant now without her presence. Correct me if I'm wrong but all three of those words essentially mean the same thing – is it a tautology? – so his literary skills may not be quite as good as he believes. He also managed to recount a joke that he had shared with Haruki Murakami at a festival in Shanghai the previous summer before shaking his head and saying 'Oh, Haruki!' with quiet delight. The joke was, of course, in Japanese and I glanced at Xi-Go Luan, who ran a debating society that my mother had been involved in for many years, and was rewarded with the expected look of bewilderment on her face.

Finally it ended, my mother was lowered down and Arthur shook my hand before pressing his cheeks against Audrey's, saying, 'Sweet girl, you can stop running now,' before moving on to greet each of the mourners individually.

'He's not coming to the pub, is he?' asked Audrey as we got back into the car.

'Probably,' I said. 'He knows which one it is anyway. And he asked me something about paparazzi earlier, so I expect that means he'll be showing up.'

'Christ on a bike,' she replied, shaking her head and looking out the window. 'What did you think anyway? Did it go all right? Would she be happy with us?'

'I think we did her proud,' I said.

'What does the word *fluguent* mean?' asked Audrey, frowning a little.

'Fluguent?'

'Arthur used it in his monologue. *Fluguent*. What does it mean?'

'I have no idea.'

'And *peripfical*?'

'Sorry, no clue.'

'What about *cordentious*?'

'Ah,' I said. 'I think that means wanker.'

'I've never heard any of those words before,' she said. 'Why does he use them, do you think? Why can't he just talk like a normal human being?'

'The answer's really in the question there, don't you think?'

'But what's wrong with him? I don't remember him being such a moron when he was younger.'

'Back when you were dating, you mean?'

'Really, Pierce? On the day of our mother's funeral?'

'Sorry.'

'He was always a little odd, I suppose. But this dose of celebrity—'

'He's *not* a celebrity,' I insisted. 'He's a writer. And not even a very good one.'

'I thought you said you hadn't read his book.'

'I skimmed through it.'

'This dose of celebrity,' she continued, 'seems to have turned him into a complete fool. How can anyone take him seriously when he carries on as he does?'

'Strangely enough, people seem to,' I said. 'His publishers must, after all. And his literary agent. He's spoken on the radio quite a few times. What do you expect? The world is full of idiots.'

We sat in silence as the streets went by. I was looking forward to a few sandwiches and a lot of alcohol.

'Are you a little jealous of Arthur?' she asked after a moment, and I turned to look at her in surprise. 'I mean yes, quite clearly, he's a total knob. But I wondered, and I'm not trying to be cruel, but do you feel envious of him? Do you look at his life and think that it might have been you?'

'Why on earth would I think that?' I asked, appalled.

'Surely the answer to that question is obvious too.'

I never talk about *The Dead Game*, my only published novel that came out to widespread indifference almost twelve years ago. Looking back, I can see that it wasn't a particularly good book but then again I was young when I wrote it and I don't believe that I got a very fair deal. My editor, Timothy Haynes, took the book on after practically every other publishing house in the UK had turned it down. It wasn't the first time any of them had heard from me either. There'd been three earlier novels, all of which had been rejected, but I'd tried something different with *The Dead Game* and somehow I'd landed a contract. Three months before my novel was published, however, Timothy left the house to work for a film production company and no one, as they say, 'owned' me any more. I was passed over to Henrietta, an editor who already had bad blood with Timothy due to their recent divorce and his decision to commence intimate sexual relations with her sister, and over the course of a single lunch together, where she went through the manuscript page by page, she uttered the phrase 'Honestly, I don't know what Tim was thinking' on at least thirty-eight occasions and I'm pretty sure she was referring to my book and not their marital issues.

'Look, it's not dreadful,' she said as we finished up, one of the better reviews that I would ultimately receive. She reached a hand across the table and placed it on mine, as if she was telling me that I might have terminal cancer but then again I might not. 'There's a lot of people out there who like this sort of thing. Although I'm not sure it will even be to their taste. But I could be proved wrong. I've been wrong about men before, after all. Anyway, it's in the schedule, so we'll go ahead and put it out there and wait and see what happens.'

Rarely has a young writer received such rapturous support from their editor and when the book was published and widely available in at least half a dozen shops, it sank without trace, an indignity that coincided with Henrietta's refusal to answer my calls or emails. I was hurt and angry; I felt humiliated. Audrey was supportive, Mother a little less so, and Father died in the middle of the farrago, which was bloody typical of him. Finally, I decided that I would not be put off and wrote *The Living Game*, an ill-advised sequel, which was returned to me with a form letter from Henrietta's assistant, telling me that it wasn't quite right for their list and that debuts weren't doing very well at the moment.

I'm not a debut, I told her in a furious reply. *You published my first novel only last year, you bunch of worthless fuckers.*

They didn't reply to that, so I called round to see whether something could be done to salvage the book but I wasn't even allowed on to the elevators and that was the end of that, which was the point when I decided to go travelling. I'd had it with publishing, resolved never to write another word, and while living in Tittmoning with my cows I realized that the reason my writing career hadn't worked out was because essentially I simply wasn't very good. Although I had one thing that a lot of disappointed novelists lack: an ability to recognize my outstanding lack of talent. This insight made my life a lot easier and somehow I got over my failure and became quite happy in my new role as Tittmoning's leading *kuhliebhabermann*, but I won't pretend that it didn't sting when I heard that Arthur, my old childhood friend Arthur, big-dicked Arthur, had sold a novel to a far more prestigious publishing house than mine and that there was a lot of buzz within the industry about it. (For some reason, I had kept up my subscription to *The Bookseller* website and even though I genuinely don't care what goes on in the literary world any more, I visit it a few times every day just to keep abreast of developments.)

What did Arthur have that I didn't have, I asked myself? Certainly not talent. On that score, we were each other's equals.

The galling thing was that I knew immediately that things would go right for him in the way that they had gone wrong for me, and when his book was published I could see in every half-assed sentence and overwritten metaphor that he was essentially a conman and all those fuckers in the publishing houses and all those cunts in the media and those bastard bitches in their book clubs sitting around talking about character development and narrative arc and empathy would just lap it up because they'd all be too fucking stupid to recognize a case of the emperor's new clothes when they saw it. They'd latch on to his worthless piece-of-shit novel and proclaim it a work of genius and the media would flock to Arthur and call him the voice of a new generation or some other tired old cliché and I'd have to spend the rest of my life listening to his cunting voice on the radio talking about the shit he produced and pretending to be self-deprecating when it was obvious to everyone that he believed they should just give him the Nobel Prize right away and save everyone a lot of time and trouble and I'd be left, like I'd always been, alone with nothing and no one and no talent and no future and no girlfriend and no media campaign and no prizes and no reason to wear a tuxedo ever and no one thinking I'd done well for myself and no one envying me and everyone who knew me when I was a kid saying hasn't Arthur achieved a lot and what's this I hear about Pierce getting involved in some scandal in Germany with a herd of cattle? And now Mother was dead on top of everything and it seemed that even she thought he could write a better eulogy than me, the author of *The Dead Game*, who *Time Out* had once called 'possibly a novelist to keep an eye on in the future in case he produces something more interesting'. Fuck that shit.

'No,' I said to Audrey, looking at her as if I'd never been asked anything so stupid in my entire life. 'Why on earth would I be jealous of Arthur?'

*

The wake ended with a song, Arthur singing a piece he had composed for the occasion called 'The Bride of Battlerea' on a bizarre instrument called a Chinese erhu, a long-necked monstrosity that resembled a pooper-scooper, with two pegs at the top and a set of strings hanging down into a sound-box. Why he chose this title is anyone's guess, for there is no such place and if there is – which there isn't – Mother did not come from there. But there isn't anyway, so it makes no difference. Although it would be unfair of me not to admit that his voice was at least passable. There were even one or two people who appeared to be wiping tears from their eyes.

Mrs Burton, our next-door neighbour while I was growing up, laid a hand on my elbow as she spoke to me. I hadn't been able to look her in the eye for many years for her bedroom was on the other side of the wall to mine and when I was fourteen she took me aside on the street and said that she could hear everything I was doing in there when I went to bed, that I was a filthy little so-and-so and if I didn't stop I'd go blind and she'd tell my mother the reason why. It made me happy to see how wrinkled her face had become.

'It comes for us all, doesn't it?' she said.

'What does?' I asked.

'Death.'

'I suppose so,' I replied. 'It might be your turn next.'

'Or yours,' she said. *'Be on the alert then, for you do not know the day nor the hour.* Matthew. Chapter 25. Verse 13.'

'That's a cheerful thought,' I said.

'I suppose you'll be selling the house now?' she asked anxiously.

'I hadn't given it much thought,' I said. 'I'll have to speak to Audrey, of course. It belongs to both of us.'

'You won't be letting it out, will you?'

'I don't know,' I replied. 'As I said, that is a conversation which has yet to take place.'

'Do you remember William Hart, Mrs Hart's son from number thirteen?'

'I do,' I said. 'Vividly.' William Hart was a tough little bastard who had bloodied my nose on more than one occasion during my formative years and, at my tenth birthday party, had threatened to urinate in my ear if I didn't give him my brand-new Spirograph. He had a dog, an incredibly violent mongrel that answered to the name of Princess Margaret-Rose, who was mortal enemies with my own dog, Chester, although they did, of course, occasionally fornicate with each other. Not too different to humans in that regard, I suppose.

'Well, when she died, William rented the house out.' She glanced around in case she might be overheard and lowered her voice as she pulled me so close that I could see the dusty moustache that rested above her upper lip. 'To a Pakistani family, if you please,' she told me. 'They're very nice, of course. I'd have nothing bad to say about any of them but still. You wouldn't do something like that, would you?'

'When Audrey and I decide,' I assured her, 'you will be the first to know.'

'Thank you,' she said, apparently relieved by this assurance. 'Of course I'm not racist,' she added. 'You know that, Pierce, don't you?'

'I do, of course.'

'I just don't like Pakistani people. Or Indians. Or Sri Lankans. Or anyone from that part of the world, if I'm honest.'

'I understand,' I said, although I didn't.

'You know, he's one of them now.'

'Who's one of what?' I asked, confused.

'William Hart,' she told me. 'He's one of them.'

'He's a Pakistani?' I asked. 'How on earth did he manage that?'

'No, don't be ridiculous,' she said, slapping my arm and laughing. 'How could that ever happen? No, he's a homosexual.' She lowered her voice even more so it was almost a whisper. 'Don't say anything. It wouldn't be fair on him.'

Arthur had come to the end of his song by now and I could see him walking towards me with two glasses of champagne in his hands, a curious choice I thought for a wake.

'Mrs Burton,' he said, smiling at her. 'I can't believe you're still alive.'

'Oh you!' she said, blushing like a schoolgirl.

'Mrs Burton was just telling me that William Hart is a Pakistani now,' I said.

Arthur frowned and scratched his face, as if he felt there was a joke in there somewhere but he couldn't get to the bottom of it.

'I'll love you and leave you,' said Mrs Burton, holding

my right hand in her left, and Arthur's left hand in her right, so we formed an unholy fellowship. 'I'm sorry for your loss, both of you.'

I felt irritated. Where was Arthur's loss? The mother of a boy he had known many years ago had died; I failed to see how he was an immediate representative of grief.

'Audrey looks well,' he said when it was just the two of us again. 'For her age, I mean.'

'She's two years younger than you.'

'Do you know what you're going to do with the house?' he asked.

'Not you as well.'

He shrugged. 'It's a fairly common question at these affairs, isn't it? I never know what to say at them.'

'And so you descend into cliché. What a surprise.'

He raised an eyebrow and waited a long time before speaking again, sipping his champagne and looking around the room, hoping to be recognized. There was a nineteen-year-old boy, bespectacled, clearly a student, working behind the bar and he settled his eyes on him. Superman's X-ray beams could not have penetrated any deeper. There was a good chance that sooner or later the boy would approach him, which would give him a chance to refuse a photo.

'Are you familiar with the German word *micschetell-feiffer*?' he asked me after a moment.

'I am,' I said. 'It means *a collection of German-sounding syllables rolled together that have absolutely no meaning at all but sound authentic to a person of below average intelligence*.'

'Not quite,' he replied. 'Perhaps in some of the more

remote Bavarian regions, that's how they define it. But in general it's a term used for a man who has not succeeded in his goals, perhaps through no fault of his own, but who resents those who have and so looks down his nose at them, making sarcastic observations and assuming that the target of his resentment is too stupid to understand him.'

'Incredible how so much can be said by so little,' I replied. 'Those Germans, eh?'

'And the word for the unwitting recipient of so much jealousy and approbation is known as a *kelshtving*.' He smiled at me and I felt a corrosive mixture of anger, envy and humiliation course through my veins.

'I suppose you're telling me that you're the *kelshtving*,' I said. 'And I'm the *micschetellfeiffer*.'

'I'm not telling you anything of the sort,' said Arthur with a shrug. 'I'm simply talking with an old friend at the funeral of his mother.' He glanced at his watch. 'But unfortunately, like Mrs Burton, I too will have to love you and leave you. My desk awaits me. My fountain pen is pulsating with anticipation. My blank white pages are moist with the knowledge that soon they will be filled. Perhaps we'll see each other soon?'

'Would you like to go outside and compare penis sizes?' I asked. 'Just for old time's sake, I mean?'

He frowned and shook his head.

'Some other time then?'

'Probably not,' he said.

He made his way out the door just as Audrey came over, her face a little drawn from the emotion of the day.

'Was that Arthur leaving?' she asked. She looked disappointed and for a moment I thought she was going to start crying. 'I should have said goodbye. We under-estimated him, didn't we? What he said by the graveside . . . Mother would have been very moved.'

'Well he's probably still out in the car park if you want to run after him,' I said. 'You can pick up where you left off in the Burlington.'

'Shut up. I confided in him earlier that I'd argued with Mother the night she died and that I've been feeling rotten about it ever since.'

'You were always arguing,' I pointed out. 'It would only be news if you'd ended things on good terms.'

'But it was over something so stupid.'

'Really? What was it, a soap opera? A recipe? A knitting pattern?'

'Yes, Pierce, it was a combination of all those things be-cause while you've been over there in Germany getting yourself in trouble with the law for shagging cows, that's *all* Mother and I ever discussed. Recipes, knitting patterns and *Coronation Street.*'

I ignored the first part of her speech; far too much of my life had already been spent offering a perfectly sensible explanation for something that others insist on seeing in the most perverted manner. 'Well aren't you going to tell me?' I asked finally.

'Tell you what?'

'What it was that you were arguing about.'

'I told you. It was something stupid. Something unim-portant.'

'Can you be a little clearer?'

'Fine,' she said with a deep put-upon sigh. 'We were arguing over you.'

'Over me?'

'Well, not so much over you as over your book.'

'What book?'

'*The Dying Game.*'

'Oh, that book.' I felt a little surprised. No one had uttered those three words to me for many years. 'What about it?'

'She said that Arthur had been to see her once and they'd got into a conversation about it and she'd said that she thought it was quite good actually and he'd said no, it wasn't quite good at all, it was *very* good, but that you hadn't stuck with it because you had expected the world to be handed to you on the day it was published. He said that if you'd been a little less arrogant, then things might have gone differently for you. You mightn't have ended up screwing cattle in Tittmoning.'

'I haven't ended up anywhere yet,' I said quietly.

'Anyway, I said that it was for the best, that there was only pain and torture associated with that world, a constant feeling of under-appreciation, and she said that she'd said something similar to Arthur and he told her that the only way to survive it was to put on a front, to present yourself as a genius. That if you did that, then others might take you seriously too. Just wear them down. Then you could lead the life you wanted to lead.'

'Deep,' I said, draining my champagne and deciding to

make like a Scotsman and get a drink for each hand. 'He should put that in his next book.'

'Perhaps he will,' she said sharply. 'It's more than you'll do though, isn't it?'

I returned to Tittmoning the following week and over the course of a busy two days reacquainted myself with Bess, Carla, Daphne, Jezebel, Rachel, Shirley, Kate, Arabella, Madonna and – yes, I admit it – Kurt. They seemed pleased enough to see me although, to be fair, cattle, like members of the Royal Family, don't tend to go in for outward displays of affection. On the flight across, I glanced at the books my fellow travellers were holding, convinced that one of them would be reading Arthur's novel and that this would provide some sort of poetic ending to my trip, but I was disappointed. Although in fairness, very few of them were reading books at all. At least not as I understand the term. And certainly nothing by Arthur. Or by me. Not that that was a surprise as I'd been out of print for many years. But still it made me happy that no one was reading his work. So far, after all, he'd only published a single book, which was something that we had in common. And even if people were paying attention to it there was nothing to say that he would ever write another one. Or, if he did, that it would be accepted for publication. Or, if it was, that it would get good reviews. Or, if it should, that it would catch on with the public. Or, if it happened to, that it would stand the test of time. He would be exactly where I was, flying into Salzburg airport, looking forward to getting back into my lederhosen and refamiliarizing myself with the comforting smells of unpasteurized milk.

Perhaps I would even be the boss of him then. Perhaps I would show him the ropes and introduce him to my friends in Der Glockenspiel pub and he would be my sidekick, a boy who didn't define me by ridiculous and unsubstantiated rumours. Here comes Arthur, the locals would say as he wandered down the road. He was never supposed to achieve anything in life but somehow, against all the odds, he made a brief success once, failed to capitalize on it, but became a man who has learned to reconcile failure with an unremittingly positive attitude towards the world.

Or – as they say in Germany – a *schleinermetzenmann*.

Empire Tour

The straining sound of a crane's jib being extended. The thump of hammers, steel against steel. The shriek of the soldering irons. The insistent pounding of last night's champagne behind her eyes. Agatha inched her foot back a little in the bed, hoping to make contact with Archie's leg, but he wasn't there and the sheets were cool to the touch. A terrible sinking feeling in her stomach. She sat up, turned and examined his pillow, her fingers moving lightly across the satin. It was slightly distressed but not terribly so. Had he come to bed at all? Had he come to bed *here*?

She rose, naked, unsteady on her feet, and stepped over towards the window, parting the curtains slightly to look across the harbour. She longed to see the streets of London, the rain spooling in the gaps between the cobblestones, the filth choking the gutters. Instead, over there was the cool blue tide of Sydney Cove as it flowed towards Circular Quay and over here were hundreds of black-smeared workmen engaged on one interminable task: building their terrible bridge.

It had not been her idea to travel so far from England,

that was all down to Archie. She would have preferred to stay at home but everyone in their circle had undertaken an Empire Tour at some point in their lives and they'd never even travelled outside England together. It didn't look good.

'Isn't it just for honeymooners?' she asked him, reluctant to leave their child and her writing for so long. 'Couldn't we just take a week by the lakes instead?'

'We couldn't afford an Empire Tour when we got married,' he told her. 'Not on my salary alone. But now? Things are different, aren't they? Your little books are selling. My business is growing. All that money just sitting in the bank, waiting for someone to do something frivolous with it.'

'But does it really make sense to squander our savings when we're both perfectly content here in England?'

'You might be content,' he said, settling down with a cigarette, a gin and tonic and a Dorothy L. Sayers, a novelist he read whenever he was in a passive-aggressive mood. 'I need some fun.'

There was nothing she could say to that. She knew that Archie had been bored ever since he left the air force and began working in business, that all-encompassing but ill-defined term. Occasionally she would ask him what it was that he actually did every day and he would reply, 'Oh, a bit of this, a bit of that, it brings in the shekels, doesn't it?' And she had to admit that it did. He was doing quite well for himself now, far better than he ever had when he was a pilot. Although not as well as she. She was, to use a vulgarity that Archie adored, coining it in. And still he was bored. A distance had grown between them.

She agreed that they might take six months abroad, a prospect she dreaded, and Rosalind was duly sent to stay with Clara, Agatha's mother, with very little fuss on either of their parts. They sailed to Calais and took the Orient Express to Venice, where they argued for a week. Archie complained of how the Italians insisted on speaking Italian, while Agatha, forgetting a wide-brimmed hat one afternoon, suffered a sunburn on her shoulders and had her purse stolen in the Piazza San Marco. They were glad to move on, continuing east to Athens, then a ship to Egypt, a cruise along the Nile and a train journey across Mesopotamia. To her surprise, Agatha had liked all these places, with their welcoming people, unfamiliar languages and colourful bazaars. She bought a set of notebooks and started to write down the sights and sounds that she observed, thinking that one day she might be able to use some of them in a novel. Might her detective not find himself sailing down the Nile one day too? And if so, might a murder not take place for him to investigate? The boat that she and Archie sailed on held an eclectic group of people and she overheard many intriguing conversations. Characters were appearing in her head in search of a story, like guests arriving at a party where they only vaguely knew the host.

She longed to be at home where she could concentrate.

Asia did not prove quite so much of a success. Pakistan, India, Burma, Siam: these places excited Archie but frightened her. There were so many people. Animals on the streets, the pink-tongued dogs walking with their heads bowed low, copulating in public. Children with missing limbs, enormous eyes staring at her in pitiful desperation. Men and women emptying their bowels in narrow laneways. And the heat, the heat, the heat. Always the heat. At times she felt something approaching terror.

In the East Indies, they stayed with Major Blenchley, an old school friend of Archie's, in a tumbledown, sprawling shack that had pretensions to respectability. Archie and the Major spent most of their days big-game shooting, leaving Agatha and the Major's wife, Norma, together on the porch, struggling to make small talk. Norma was a wisp of a thing, lacking any confidence whatsoever, living in fear of her bloated brute of a husband whose bulbous nose was capillaried with red veins. She confided in Agatha how she had suffered eight miscarriages over eight years and seemed overly interested in Rosalind, asking questions that all seemed to have one subtext: *how could you leave her?*

There were other women there too, native women, and Agatha observed moments between the Major and several of their number that bordered on the scandalous. Seated alone with a book in their stifling lounge one afternoon she overheard him in the porch telling his man-servant that Archie had married an ugly woman with a fine body while he had married a beautiful woman with a terrible body and so they were both miserable with their lot. 'Mrs Blenchley's face with Mrs Christie's body,' he said laughing, 'that's what I want,' and the manservant laughed along saying, 'Yes, Sahib, quite right, Sahib, very funny, Sahib.' She had been very happy to leave.

And then it was on to Australia.

They arrived in Perth and, although everyone knew that Australians were brutes, she almost felt as if she was among civilized people again. But the further she got from home, the more depressed she grew. Still, the people were friendly, too friendly she thought at times, and couldn't suffer any class distinction, unlike the Indians, who resented their British overlords but seemed to venerate them at the same time.

Archie had some connection with the brother of the Governor-General, who took them for a day trip around King's Park, where they picnicked in sight of the Swan. The menthol scent of the eucalyptus trees in their nostrils led to an unsuccessful hunt for sleeping koalas. The brother, whose name was Greene, flirted with Agatha so much that she rather enjoyed it, particularly since this Greene fellow was young and handsome and some sort of local celebrity for his abilities on the tennis court. Throughout their back and forth, she glanced at Archie, wondering whether he was annoyed by her flirting, but he seemed scarcely to notice, so intent was he in talking to Greene's sister, Charlotte, who had come along to make up a foursome and was of equally good stock as her beautiful brother.

'Archie,' said Agatha at one point. 'Mr Greene says he should like to take me dancing some night. Can you bear a scandal?' She smiled at him, uncertain what response she was hoping to elicit.

'Sounds like a fine idea, my dear,' he replied. 'But only if Greene allows me to take the same liberty with his sister. What do you say, Miss Greene? Would you care to go dancing with a retired pilot some night?'

'I don't see what the fact that you used to be a pilot has to do with anything,' said Agatha.

'Don't you fly any more then?' asked Miss Greene who, in Agatha's opinion, was a trollop. The manner in which she had painted her face and her fingernails and toenails testified to that; the woman was little more than a canvas with breasts.

'Oh, I try to make it into the skies whenever I can,' said Archie, leaning back on an elbow in an insouciant manner and saying this as if most people jumped into a cockpit and flew a few thousand feet in the air whenever they felt the slightest urge. 'But it's difficult, you know. Time presses terribly. My work commitments keep me awfully busy.'

'What is it that you do exactly, Mr Christie?'

'I'm in business.'

'Which means what?'

'That's what I'd like to know,' said Agatha, interrupting her. 'Men use the term "business" as a catch-all for everything, don't you find? We women don't know what they get up to.'

'I don't find that at all, actually,' replied Miss Greene, picking a piece of tobacco from between her two front teeth and examining the flake before flicking it away. She smoked malodorous concoctions that she rolled between thin papers. The woman was vulgarity personified. 'Most men of my acquaintance who engage in business have a very clear way of expressing what they do.'

'I shouldn't like to bore you,' said Archie.

'I'd walk away if you did.'

'Look here, Agatha,' said Greene, laughing and shaking his head. 'You want to mind your house. My sister here has a habit of running off with married men.'

'Only if they've got one foot out the door already,' said Miss Greene, slapping him on the arm. 'Don't listen to a word he says, Agatha. Aren't brothers awful? Do you have a brother?'

'One,' said Agatha. 'Monty.'

'He's a drunk,' added Archie in a distracted tone as he rooted in the picnic basket for another snack. Agatha stared at him, appalled that he would make such a remark in front of strangers.

'I like a man who's a drunk,' said Miss Greene. 'I knew a chap once, teetotal, and he was a frightful bore. The advantage of a drunk is that he's always looking for fun. Not to mention the fact that he never gets out of bed until the middle of the afternoon, which is an advantage for me as I can't bear to be spoken to before noon.'

'And how would you know what time any man gets out of bed?' asked Archie with a smile.

'I have my ways.'

'I'm sure you do.'

'Isn't it warm?' asked Agatha.

'Men are frightful sloths, of course. They'd spend all day in bed if they could. They'd only rise at cocktail hour to put on their evening wear and go out on a seduction.'

'You have a low opinion of us, I think, Miss Greene,' said Archie.

103

'I do, it's true,' she replied, considering it. 'I should be more like my friend Miss Jameson. She has cut men out of her life entirely and seems all the happier for it.'

'Did she cut them out or did they never cut her in?' he asked. 'Miss Jameson sounds to me like an ugly girl with a crooked eye and a hump.'

'Quite wrong there, old chap,' said Greene, sitting up. 'She's a beauty. Everyone used to be mad about her. It seems that her tastes lie elsewhere though.'

'Elsewhere? How do you mean?'

'Think about it,' replied Greene quietly, a smirk spreading across his face.

'You don't mean that she's a deviant?' asked Archie, his eyes opening wide.

'Yes, I suppose I do.'

'How intriguing. I'd love to meet her. We met a deviant at a party once in London, didn't we, Agatha? Awful creature. Smelled like the dead. Wore trousers. I thought they were all like that but from the sounds of things I've got it wrong. Perhaps they're different in Australia. What do you think, Agatha? Would you like to meet this Miss Jameson?'

Agatha looked away and said nothing. She longed to be away from Greene and his horrible sister and this terrible park and their awful conversation. She wanted to be back in her hotel room; she wanted Archie to look at her in such a way that said that he wanted that too.

'I'm growing tired,' she said finally. 'Shall we go back soon, Archie?'

'Not quite yet,' he replied.

An argument ensued that night. The trip to Perth was cut short and they took an ocean liner across the Great Australian Bight, docking for a few days at Nullarbor National Park before moving on to Adelaide, where Agatha attended a recital alone, before agreeing to a week in Tasmania, where they stayed at a rather nice hotel in Hobart. There, a reconciliation of sorts took place over excellent fish suppers. But of course they knew no one in Hobart and there was no society whatsoever, so they could rub along as if it was old times. It was not a large city and every day they woke late before making their way to the harbour for lunch and a stroll around the parks, settling down in a quiet spot to read or snooze the afternoon away. They made love once in the shade of some trees, scandalous behaviour, but Archie had been in the mood and Agatha didn't want to say no; she'd longed for his touch for so long but there, beneath the Mountain Ash of the Queen's Domain, she felt only a self-conscious terror, certain that a park ranger might appear to arrest them. Still, there was a sense of the idyllic about the island and she began to wonder whether the problems in their marriage might not be disappearing.

But then came New South Wales.

They had been here a week already and, although Agatha had tried to keep the spirit of Tasmania alive, the distance between her and Archie had grown once again.

He knew someone in Sydney too, of course, and it was at a party at the chap's house that they had first

105

encountered Mrs Crossley, a widowed neighbour. 'Too young to have buried a husband,' his friend remarked when he pointed her out across the room.

'And too beautiful not to have found another,' replied Archie, staring at her as if she was the only thing of value in the room, despite the fact that his own wife was standing next to him.

Mrs Crossley was not a flirt, not in the same way that Miss Greene of Perth had been, but she clearly enjoyed the attentions of men and knew that she could reel them in and make them entirely hers before deciding whether she wanted to set them free again or keep a tight hold. Agatha watched as most of the men present attempted to make their way with her, and how she would allow it for a time, smiling, engaging in conversation, locking her eyes with theirs to imply that, yes, she just might, if the moment came along, before transferring her attentions to someone else.

'You seemed to get along very well with Mrs Crossley tonight,' Agatha remarked as they changed for bed later that evening.

'Mrs Crossley?' asked Archie, furrowing his brow as if he was trying to remember exactly who she was, a display of such amateur theatricality that Agatha felt embarrassed for him. 'Yes, she seemed pleasant enough. Handsome woman, isn't she?'

'If you like that sort of thing,' said Agatha.

'I imagine that most men would like that sort of thing,' said Archie. 'Most unmarried men, that is,' he added, correcting himself and looking across at his wife with a smile. She smiled back, for that was all it took to restore him to her good graces. The truth was that she loved him in a way that she had never thought possible. And it never subsided, never diminished, never scarred. Despite the way he treated her.

They stayed in Sydney longer than originally planned, taking a small apartment at Milson's Point where Mrs Crossley became a regular visitor. At first, she came on the pretext of seeing Agatha but gradually it became clear that she was hoping to run into Archie, and Archie would remain at home waiting to see her too. And so they would sit, the three of them on their balcony, drinking freshly made lemonade and watching the workers on the ground below building their bridge.

'What do you think of it anyway?' asked Archie, nodding in the direction of the plot of land that had been cleared to take the foundations.

'It's much needed,' said Mrs Crossley. 'For any of us living on this side of the water, the crossing is a nightmare. The ferries are always overcrowded and of course they'll let absolutely anybody on. No, I shall be very happy when it's finished. Although it will take years, no doubt, and I will be in my dotage by the time I can cross it for the first time.'

'Nonsense,' said Archie, laughing and shaking his head. 'A woman like you should never grow old.'

'What on earth does that mean?' asked Agatha irritably. 'How could she not grow old? And what type of woman *should* grow old, since you are deciding upon this re-order of nature?'

'Steady on, old girl,' said Archie, blushing slightly. 'It was only a joke.'

Shortly after this, Mrs Crossley had stopped coming to visit. There had been no argument, no falling-out, no incident that merited a cooling of the air; she had simply stopped calling. And despite the fact that Agatha had no desire whatsoever to spend time with her, she continued to send invitations but these came back with polite refusals.

Agatha liked to wander the streets of the Rocks in the afternoons, enjoying the narrow laneways with their ramshackle shops and tightly packed workers' houses. One afternoon, a burst of heat and a near-fainting spell led her through the open frontage of a public house, self-conscious but desperate for something that might cool her down. The sign said 'Fortune of War' and inside, away from the sun, her confidence grew and she stood at the bar, looked the man in the eye and ordered a schooner of pale Australian beer. Taking it into the half-empty backroom, she engaged in some people-watching: a young couple, sitting close together and whispering confidences; a middle-aged man, unshaven and wearing a distressed expression, seated beneath the ANZAC sign; a woman going through the local newspaper and circling a page bearing the headline 'Honest Girls Wanted'.

A noise from the bar made her glance outside and she saw a group of six young men, Aborigines, laughing loudly with the barman as he placed beers on the counter before them all. They were bridge workers; Agatha could tell from the way they were dressed. She watched them carefully, the ease they took in each other's company, the way they threw their heads back and laughed. Her eyes settled on a young man of about twenty whose shirt was open halfway down his chest. She could see the curve of his musculature and felt a desire to touch that dark skin, to feel the smooth tautness of it. Her eyelids fluttered a little as an image came to her mind – her lips against the boy's bare brown breast – and she swallowed as he turned to look at her, his eyes a fierce blue, his nose fleshy at the nostrils, his tongue pink as it emerged from his mouth and gathered the beer suds from his upper lip in a slow sensual gesture. Unsteady on her feet, she rose, leaving her drink unfinished, and walked towards him; in the narrow space between the front and back bar he stepped aside to let her pass. Her shoes slipped on a spillage and she almost collided with him, their bodies close together for a moment as she looked in his face. He smelled awful and wonderful. The man beneath the ANZAC sign watched them, ready to pounce. 'Steady, missus,' said the young Aborigine, and she felt a shiver run through her body as she moved forward, back out on to the street, where the heat overtook her again. She thought she might tear her clothes off and run naked down George Street, screaming in delight. But, of course, she didn't.

Archie made no reference to the disappearance of Mrs Crossley and Agatha thought to bring it up one day, to ask why he thought Mrs Crossley had dropped them so suddenly, but in the end she decided against it. She didn't want to hear his answer.

But now, this morning, it was almost impossible not to suspect the worst. She turned away from her observation of the progress of the bridge and went around to Archie's side of the bed, burying her face in his pillow, trying to define by scent whether or not he had slept there the night before.

It was an extraordinary thing, of course, for a husband and wife not to retire together from a party – it was not the sort of thing that would ever happen in London – but it was exactly what had taken place the previous night. They had been invited to the home of the Forsters, a couple who lived only a short walk from their apartment, and had strolled down together in the late evening to join a very jolly party. Agatha was having a wonderful time, particularly because Archie was being so solicitous of her, but then they had both turned at the same moment and caught the eye of Mrs Crossley across the room. The lady froze visibly for a moment, her expression set in stone, before relaxing her features and adopting what Agatha defined as a practised expression. Archie, holding Agatha's elbow, tensed, swallowed and said nothing. The tableau was quite extraordinary, Agatha felt. The three of them locked together in some ridiculous way, no one willing to be the first to say or do anything.

'Look,' said Agatha finally, the word catching in her throat. 'Look who it is.'

'Of course,' said Archie, and now Mrs Crossley advanced towards them both, wrapping them up in a flurry of kisses and self-admonishments for not seeing them more frequently.

'I've just been so busy of late,' she explained. 'I intended to write but never found an opportunity. My brother came to visit, you see, from Canberra.'

'I didn't know you had a brother,' said Agatha coolly.

'Oh yes.'

'What's his name?'

Mrs Crossley stared at her, her expression fixed, but then she smiled a little. 'His name is John,' she said. 'He's the member for Darwin so splits his time between the Northern Territories and the capital. You can look him up in the Members' Directory if you don't believe me.'

Agatha flushed scarlet. 'Of course not,' she said. 'Naturally I didn't mean—'

'And how are you, Archie?' said Mrs Crossley, turning her attentions to Agatha's husband. 'You have quite a colour these days. Been spending a lot of time outdoors, have you? You always seemed more the indoors type to me.'

'Well, yes, a bit, I suppose,' muttered Archie.

'You promised to lend me that book, didn't you? The history of the Indian subcontinent that you praised so highly. But you never did. I should be very cross with you.'

'I do apologize,' said Archie, and Agatha noticed how he was unable to meet her eye. 'I could get a boy to bring it over tomorrow if you like.'

'A boy?' she said, staring at him and waiting for so long before continuing that Agatha hoped the ground would open and swallow them all up. 'How terribly thoughtful,' she said finally. 'Agatha, you have a terribly thoughtful husband, do you know that?'

'Yes, of course,' said Agatha miserably.

'A man of real integrity and honour. He'd never let a lady down. Would you, Archie?'

'Now look here, Sarah,' began Archie, and Agatha started, for she had never heard him use her Christian name before.

'Oh but look, here come Mr Zéla and his nephew,' said Mrs Crossley, her voice raising in delight as she looked towards the doorway. 'I must go over and say hello.' She nodded at them both politely and moved off, leaving husband and wife alone together, a phrase that until now Agatha had always considered to be oxymoronic.

The rest of the evening passed in some sort of nightmare. They couldn't look at each other, couldn't speak. They made conversation with other couples and pretended that they were not suffering. And then, quite late in the evening, Agatha emerged from the ladies' room, took a wrong turn on to an unexpected corridor and in the gloom ahead saw Archie and Mrs Crossley standing there, locked in some position of combat, he holding on to her arm as she pulled away from him, pointing her finger at his face before turning and disappearing out of sight, a direction in which he followed her, away from Agatha's viewpoint. She didn't know what to do. Should she stay where she was? Return to the party? Follow them wherever they had gone and cause a scene?

In the end, she did nothing at all, simply lost herself

in the back and forth of the guests once again, and when Archie finally reappeared she told him that she had a sick headache and wanted to go home.

'All right,' he said. 'You don't mind walking?'

'Of course not. It's only two minutes away.'

'I might stay a little longer,' he said, looking directly at her now as if he was challenging her to accuse him of something. 'You don't mind, do you?'

'Why should I mind?' she replied. 'Of course you must stay. I'll see you later.'

And with that she had said goodnight to her hosts and returned to their apartment, stripped naked and thrown herself on to the bed, where she wept like a child and finally fell asleep in a tangle of sheets.

But now it was the next day. And she didn't know whether he had come back at all. But he must have, mustn't he? He couldn't have stayed away all night. It was entirely possible that he had climbed into bed and she had simply failed to hear him. This had happened before, after all. Many times. But would he really have risen early too? That seemed unlikely.

The door opened and there he was, wearing his day clothes. She glanced towards the wardrobe; last night's suit must be in there.

'All right, old girl?' he asked, barely glancing at her, despite the fact that not only had she omitted to put her nightdress on before going to bed but she hadn't bothered to wear it this morning either and was standing bare by the window as the sun poured in behind her.

Mrs Blenchley's face with Mrs Christie's body, the Major had said. But then Sydney, this magnificent city of Sydney, was always so damned hot that Agatha wondered why anyone bothered with clothes at all. It was a miracle that more of the natives didn't simply pass out as they made their way to and from their places of business. It was astonishing that the dogs in the street didn't lay down on the scorching pavements and beg for the whole miserable business of existence to come to an end once and for all.

Australia. The fact was that if they went any further west they would be on their way home again. There was that to look forward to. There was that much at least.

Haystack Girl

Auntie Dolly phoned to say that Lizzie had turned up out of the blue a few hours earlier, seeking sanctuary. That was the exact phrase she used, as if my sister was a deposed queen in a Tudor novel. I felt a hot rage burning inside me when I thought about how much she must have spent to get across there. Flights don't come cheap and then there's the cost of the bus up to Dublin Airport, the Tube from Heathrow to Colliers Wood and a taxi over to Auntie Dolly's flat after that. I'd been over there myself the previous summer and my wallet was nearly empty by the time I fell in the door. Mam had said it was best if I spent a few weeks in London as she couldn't stand the sight of me. She and Lizzie blamed me for everything that had happened, which was not a bit fair. Anyway, over I went but Auntie Dolly sent me home after five days. She said there was something wrong with me, that I was a peculiar article.

An old man winked at me on the Tube while I was there, somewhere between Balham and Tooting Bec. I was wearing short trousers and he was looking at my legs. I winked right back and made kissy faces at him. That fairly silenced him, the old perv. He stood up and walked further down the carriage to interfere with someone else. I followed him along and sat down next to him, grinning like a mad thing and putting on my sexy voice. 'Was there something you wanted?' I asked. 'Or do you just have a funny eye?'

'I'm sorry,' he said, looking down at his ratty old runners. 'Leave me alone, please.' Anyway, I left him alone.

Lizzie's flit only bothered me because she owed me twenty euros. She'd owed it to me for more than a month because I, in my generosity, had lent it to her on the understanding that I'd get twenty-two back within the week but I hadn't seen a penny since then. She claimed poverty every time I demanded payment and yet somehow she'd managed to get herself all the way from Wexford to London without any trouble. I wasn't too happy about that, I can tell you.

Mam threw a conniption fit when she got the call.

'She's what? She's where? She can't be! Well how did she get there? What do you mean she took a plane, what kind of a plane? Is she all right? Does she have money? How long is she staying? Did she remember her warm cardigan?'

This went on and on. I was sitting at the top of the stairs, eating a Curly Wurly and having a great laugh over it. This was before I remembered the twenty euros that Lizzie owed me; I laughed no more after that. Mam took the name of the Lord our God in vain about fifty times and started crying. Then she started screaming. Then she started crying again. Then she said something in Irish that I didn't understand. And then she said something that sounded a bit like Russian.

'My children will be the death of me,' she declared finally. 'As if it's not hard enough being left alone with the pair of them, now they are literally trying to drive me into my grave. I should just take a breadknife and stab myself through my heart. It's the only thing that would make either of them happy.'

The dramatics.

To be honest, I thought it was probably for the best that Lizzie had skipped off across the water. It would give things a chance to blow over. I was surprised that Mam had even answered the phone when it rang. She'd said the previous night that she wasn't going anywhere near it from now on as it was only scumbag journalists on the other end wanting a quote and what could she say that would satisfy any of them? 'They're describing a girl I don't know,' she told me, sitting at the kitchen table with mascara running down her cheeks as she made solid headway through a Superquinn Banoffee. 'I don't recognize this creature they're talking about, do you?'

I did, certainly. Sure I know what my sister is like.

After the phone call, I went into Lizzie's room, opened her wardrobe and had a good snoop around. I'd never have done anything like this if she'd been in the house. She'd have murdered me. There were still a lot of clothes in there, all the slutty stuff that she'd bought after Dad left, so I assumed that she'd decided to go classy from now on. Either that or she thought she could buy even sluttier things in London. Her laptop was still there, sitting on the desk. It made sense that she'd left that behind. The last thing she needed was to go online and see what people were saying about her. I couldn't find her phone but she probably threw that away. A life disconnected from the Internet, that was what lay in store for her if she wanted to maintain her sanity. Imagine it! I can't. I like to know what's going on in the world.

I picked up one of her soft toys, some sort of hybrid of a bear and a dog, and had a sniff of it. It smelled of her perfume and, for a moment, I felt bad. But that moment passed quick enough.

'No, I don't want to speak to her.'

This was Mam again, back on the phone to Auntie Dolly.

'Listen, I didn't throw her out but if she wants to go, there's nothing I can do about it.'

Still Mam.

'Sure I haven't left the house in four days, Dolly. I have to get the food delivered. What? The Murphy lad brings it. No, of course not, I have to give him three euros. I doubt I'll ever be able to go outside again. And Danny's been off school ever since it started.'

True enough. But this was a Sunday and Mam had already told me that I was going back the next day, no arguments. I wasn't looking forward to it. I knew everyone would be laughing at me. I was usually good at brazening things out but this was something different. They'd be on my back, every last one of them. There was a chance that I'd even start crying and make a holy show of myself. If that happened, I thought, then I'd just go and drown myself in the Slaney. That'd learn them.

I only know one other set of twins, also brother and sister, but they're freaks, the pair of them. Their father runs the funeral parlour in town and I call them The Smileys on account of how they're always going around with big stupid grins on their faces, as if the world is a wonderful place and no one lies or cheats. They're the same age as Lizzie and me – sixteen – and all the lads in my class say they do it with each other because they hold hands when they're walking into school together and she looks a bit like a boy and he looks a bit like a girl. And I've seen them kissing too. On the cheek, now, not the lips, but still and all. I wouldn't kiss Lizzie if my life depended on it. I'd rather kiss my granny and my granny's dead.

I've known The Smileys all my life. Lizzie and I used to play with them when we were little kids, before we realized that they were freaks, and then we refused to go over there any more. Once, one of The Smileys – they're indistinguishable to me – asked could s/he see my mickey and I ran away and hid in a cardboard box and Lizzie had to come and get me to bring me home. Dad said I had to be nice to them because Daddy Smiley was his best friend but I said did it not look a bit mad that the only two sets of twins in town were going over to each other's houses all the time and Dad said that he'd never heard such nonsense in all his life and I was to stop calling them The Smileys anyway as it was rude.

But the thing I hated most about them was that

whenever Lizzie and I were there, we got stuck playing games in the room above the funeral parlour with all the dead people staring up at us through the floorboards. I'm squeamish that way. I always closed my eyes when I was running up to the Smiley twins' bedroom but then Jimmy Halpin, who was a great pal of mine when we were eight, was laid out downstairs after he got a hit of his father's tractor and I made the mistake of going in to take a look at him in his box and passed out in fright. People always say that the dead look peaceful but Jimmy Halpin looked exactly like a lad who'd had a hit of his father's tractor. And seen it coming too. I'll never forget the expression on his face. The old rigor must have set in before they could tidy him up. Anyway, Lizzie had to come down then too and bring me outside, where she kept calling my name and shaking me till I woke up.

I thought Mammy and Daddy Smiley were a right pair of knobs for calling the twins Joseph and Josephine. At least our parents had the sense to give us completely different names. Joseph and Josephine always wore similar clothes when they were kids, masculine and feminine versions of the same outfit, although it was any-one's guess who would wear which one. And even now they seem to coordinate with each other every morning. I imagine them getting dressed for school, probably in the same room having climbed out of the bed together where they'd been kissing and doing it all night long, and Joseph saying, 'Wear the blue skirt, Josephine, it'll go great with this gorgeous shirt that I'm wearing', and Josephine saying, 'I will, Joseph, you sexy beast, now get over here till I molest you.' And then the pair of them going at it like hammer and tongs. The lad who sits next to me in class, Geoffrey Jones, who is a complete legend these days and a hero for a whole generation of Irish boys, says that he saw The Smileys doing it behind the pub one afternoon, over where they keep the recycled bottles in the big green skip, and I said I didn't believe that for a moment because there was no way that either Joseph or Josephine Smiley had any genitalia at all. For some reason he thought this was only riotous and he laughed till there were tears coming down his face and I felt as good about myself as I've ever felt in my life. They probably do have genitalia though. Everyone does, as far as I know.

Sometimes I think that I'm mean about The Smileys because they actually like each other and I'm just jealous. On account of how much Lizzie and I hate each other. Or rather how much she hates me, for personally I never had any great problem with her until after Dad left and she turned into a slut and started being nasty to me all the time, blaming me for everything that had happened when none of it was my fault, no matter what anyone says. She says I'm a selfish little bastard and that if I'd only kept my nose out, then Mam and Dad would still be together and how would I like it if someone took my mobile phone and started spreading all my secrets about. 'Sure I don't have any secrets,' I told her, and she laughed like she knew every single one of them. Mam blames me too. She blames me even more than she blames Dad, which doesn't make any sense to me at all. That's why she sent me over to London that time. She says she'd rather have known nothing and have kept her family together, and I told her that if she wanted to live as an ignoramus, that was fine, but I wouldn't be a party to such witlessness. And then she looked like she wanted to hit me.

I haven't seen Dad much since he went. He blames me too. Everyone blames me, or so it seems. But at least they can turn their attentions to someone else now that Lizzie is the laughing stock of the whole country. They're even talking about her in America. I saw a piece about her on the *Huffington Post*. They'll probably find a way to blame me for that too.

The first day back at school was just as bad as I'd expected. There were two empty seats: Lizzie's, of course. And Geoffrey's. Tommy Devlin, who I love, was in his usual spot and he was the only one who didn't burst out laughing when I walked in. Even The Smileys started giggling, their faces pressed together, probably wondering whether they could get away with snogging the heads off each other in the middle of the classroom.

As it turned out, Geoffrey had been away from school all week, just like me. His parents had taken his phone away and they'd confiscated his computer, so no one had got anywhere near him to offer their congratulations.

A few of the lads did that cough-talk thing, where you bark into your hand and then mutter something like 'Your sister's a whore' and then look all innocent afterwards as if they hadn't said a word. I'd expected that. I'd expected worse, to be honest. A lad who was always being bullied threw M&M's at my head, one by one. I'd say he was only happy that someone else was getting picked on instead of him. I'll get back at him when this is all over. Every time he threw one, I picked it up and ate it. In the end, I think I ate half his pack. So I got the last laugh there.

'You've been off for the last week, Danny?' asked Benji Dunne, who sits in the seat in front of me and has terrible spots. 'Were you helping out in the fields, was it? There's a terrible smell of hay off you.'

And then he started laughing and he high-fived the prick next to him, who said, 'Good one, Benzer, good one', the big suck-up. I'll get him too. I'll get the both of them.

When Mr Hunter came in, he seemed surprised to find me sitting there and he started blushing. The poor fella is always blushing for no reason. That's why we call him Blusher. Poor old Blusher, he's harmless really and he's had it awful rough. His wife's dead, his son's an alcoholic and his dog's got cancer. Anyway, he took one look at me, the face went scarlet, and then he turned around to write some old nonsense on the board about William Wordsworth and the spontaneous overflow of blah blah blah. That's what he does whenever he starts blushing, because then he can turn his back on us and wait until the redness goes out of his cheeks. Only we're all on to that trick and Patsy Cole said, 'Mr Hunter, look, I'm after cutting myself with my compass, there's blood everywhere!' Which meant that he had to turn around to take a look and everyone started laughing at the state of him. I didn't laugh. The poor man has an affliction and I'm not cruel in that way. Tommy Devlin didn't laugh either. Tommy Devlin would never laugh at another man's misfortune.

So anyway, Blusher's standing there and he looks like his head is going to explode and Patsy says it was all a mistake, sure he doesn't even own a compass, and then he asks Blusher what colour the traffic lights go when the cars are supposed to stop but before he could answer the door opened and in walked Geoffrey, a nervous smile on his face, and the place erupted in cheers. It was like in those gladiator films when the lads walk into the middle of that big round thing in Rome and everyone goes mental, even though they just want to see them suffer and have the heads eaten off them by lions.

'Leg! Leg! Leg! Leg! Leg!' everyone shouted, banging their fists on their desks, and that doesn't look right when I write it down. They weren't saying *leg* as in the thing between your waist and your foot. They were saying *ledge* as in short-for-legend. Geoffrey, to be fair to him, looked a bit sheepish at first but then he grinned even wider and he even gave a sort of professional bow, like he'd just come out for his curtain call and was surprised to find that the audience had hung around this long instead of going off to the lobby for a drink. He strolled down to his usual seat, practically whistling in his nonchalance, but then stopped when he saw me sitting there and, to give the lad credit, he looked a bit ashamed of himself and turned around, hoping for another empty place, but the only spare one was Lizzie's and he could hardly sit there.

He was a bit lost, poor fella. Did he think I was going to beat him up or something? Sure I haven't got a muscle anywhere on my body.

'Geoffrey,' shouted Don Wichford, who's just a blow-in as he only came over from Clare this last term so he shouldn't have been shouting at anyone until he'd earned his stripes. 'You've got hay in your hair!'

'You've got some in your arse too,' said Steven Crawley.

'You've got some in your mickey,' roared Sharon Lewis, who had officially been a slut until about four weeks before, when she'd started going out with Graham Rushe and become respectable. Everyone broke their sides laughing when she said that and Geoffrey pretended to be embarrassed but I could see that he was eating it up. He didn't want to sit down in case they stopped.

None of this is really Geoffrey's fault but I'm going to get him one day too. And when I do, he won't see it coming.

Anyway, when Sharon made that crack about Geoffrey's mickey, Blusher went even more scarlet than before and I swear I thought he might have a heart attack or spontaneously combust.

'Boys,' he said weakly. 'Girls.' But that did no good. He'd have needed a whip to tame that room.

I read somewhere that you can get an operation for blushing. If I was him, that's what I'd do. I'd save up all my money and go on up to Dublin to see the top doctor and I would hand across every penny I owned and say, 'Here, fix this for me like a good man.' I mean it's only chronic.

*

There was a right commotion going on at the house.

I was trotting along the road, feeling a little more re-laxed with every step I put between me and the school, when I saw Mam charging out to the gate, dragging this blonde-haired piece by the arm and practically launching her into the street. The blonde was asking something, holding a tape recorder out in the air to catch the reply, while a young lad standing next to her was taking photographs. I heard the front door slam as Mam disappeared back inside and when the reporter turned and saw me coming towards her, she almost levitated off the ground with excitement.

'You must be the brother,' she said, wielding her tape recorder at me like Harry Potter's wand.

'Why must I?'

'You look just like Lizzie.'

'I look nothing like her,' I said, disgusted by the very idea.

'You do so,' said the photographer. 'She's a good-looking girl.'

I turned to stare at him and for once I was a bit lost for words. Did he mean that he thought I was a good-looking boy? No one had ever said such a thing to me before and it caught me off-guard. He was good-looking himself, with curly dark hair and a bit of stubble. Really white teeth too. He half-smiled at me and I felt my stomach tumble a bit. He was probably only about six or seven years older than me too. No harm in that.

'Is it true that your sister has moved up to Dublin?'

asked the blonde, and I turned back to her, trying to compose myself.

'She's not in Dublin,' I said. 'Sure Dublin wouldn't have her. She's gone to London.'

'London, right,' she said, and I felt like a right eejit for allowing myself to get trapped like that. It was the oldest trick in the book. 'And what's in London?'

'Piccadilly Circus,' I said. 'Big Ben. Prince Harry.'

A clicking sound to my left made me turn again and there was your man, snapping away as if his life depended on it. I gave him a big smile and he took the camera away from his eyes for a moment and stared at me with what I suppose you would call an interested glance. The perv.

'My left side's better,' I said, turning around to prove my point. I would have preferred to say *take a picture, it'll last longer*, but sure he was already taking pictures, so the joke would have been lost entirely.

'I meant who does she know in London?' asked the reporter. She'd had some work done on her forehead. There was something there that wasn't quite right. A bit too Nicole Kidman, if you know what I mean.

'We have an auntie there,' I said.

'Can you give me her name?'

I thought about it for a moment. My poor auntie had done nothing to deserve any of this, even if she had thrown me out the previous summer and called me a peculiar article. The last thing she needed was the tabloids landing on her doorstep. 'I can't remember,' I said.

'You can't remember your own aunt's name?'

'I want to say . . . *Fidelma*?' I began, shrugging and smiling for the photographer, who sniggered, which practically did me in. My aunt's name isn't Fidelma at all, of course. As I've already told you, it's Dolly. Dolly Dunne.

'Do you have her address?'

'Do you really think I'd give that to you?' I asked.

'Come on, Daniel,' she said, bored now. There was something in her expression that suggested she'd rather be up there in Kildare Street lobbing grenades at the Minister for Finance than down here in the arsehole of nowhere talking to a famous slut's twin brother.

'It's Danny,' I said. 'I don't like Daniel.'

'Do you know how many hits the video has received now?'

'A fair few, I'd say.'

'Over two million worldwide.'

'There's a lot of sickos out there,' I said.

'Are you ashamed of your sister?' she asked, switching on the empathy. She must have thought I was an awful fool. 'She's your twin sister, isn't she? Do you feel embarrassed by her? Would you say that you couldn't stand to look at her right now?' I might have answered, only then she said this: 'Is Lizzie the reason your father left home?'

'Shut up, you old wagon,' I said, leaping at her, and she jumped back in fright. The photographer grabbed me and put an arm around my waist to still me. You can leave that there if you like, I thought.

'Take it easy, Danny,' he said and, Christ, I felt an urge to just let my body relax back into his and fall asleep. I didn't though. I have self-control. Which is more than I can say for my twin sister. Who is officially a slut.

'You're very angry, aren't you, Danny?' asked the blonde, putting her tape recorder back in her bag, but I didn't have time to answer for just at that moment the front door flew open and Mam stormed out to drag me back inside the house before I could say another word.

'Do *not* speak to those people,' she said, wagging a finger in my face. 'They're low-lifes, every one of them. Bottom feeders. And they'll destroy us if you give them half a chance.'

I shrugged and went upstairs. I had a desperate urge to play with Mussolini, our dog, only Mussolini was dead a year already so there was no chance of that happening. So I got into bed and had a wank over the photographer instead.

Lizzie laughed at me when I told her I was gay. She literally started laughing like I'd made some great joke.

This was about four months after Dad left and she was sitting in her room listening to some old shite on her CD player and crying. I could hear her through the walls but no matter how hard I banged, she wouldn't turn the music down or put an end to the waterworks. So I went in without knocking and there she was, sitting on the bed like a Buddha in cheap make-up, looking through old photo albums like she was in a film or something. Pictures of the four of us from years ago, when Lizzie and I were just kids. Holidays over in West Cork. The time we went to Leisureland in Galway and I fell off the slide and hit my head. Mam and Dad at the school sports day.

'Can you keep it down in here, do you think?' I asked, and she looked up at me with pure hatred in her eyes. She'd changed a lot since Dad skipped out. She'd got a tattoo on her ankle, started drinking and staying out late. Getting off with lads. Not officially a slut yet but getting there.

'You keep it down,' she said, putting the album aside and scrolling through the messages on her phone instead. 'You're such a prick, you know that?' she said after a bit. 'There's something wrong with you in your head.'

'There's something wrong with you in your head,' I repeated, mimicking her.

'Oh, stop it.'

'Oh, stop it.'

'Jesus, it's like talking to a child.'

'Jesus, it's like talking to a child.'

And then she took a paperweight off her bedside table, a big glass heavy yoke that she'd won in some stupid essay competition a couple of years before and flung it at my head. Had it hit me, I'd have been out for the count, for that thing was a weapon of mass destruction. As it was, it just grazed me, stinging my left ear as it sailed past and crashed into her wardrobe. But it gave me a terrible fright all the same. Even Lizzie looked a bit alarmed by this sudden act of violence.

I sat on the ground and put my head in my hands. I needed a moment to compose myself. I was the victim of an attempted murder. And all because I'd asked her to turn the music down.

'What's the matter with you now?' she asked, the

smallest amount of concern seeping into her voice. I'd say she felt a bit relieved that she'd missed me. She might have been up on manslaughter charges. 'Danny, are you all right? It didn't even touch you.'

Out of the blue, the tears came. They were as big a shock to me as they were to her. And the fact that I was crying made me cry even more because I was so surprised by the whole thing.

'Jesus, Danny,' she said. 'I'm sorry. I'm just so angry with you for what you did. You've never even apologized. You've never even admitted your part in it.'

'I didn't do anything,' I said, between sobs.

'Well what's wrong with you then? Stop crying, for fuck's sake!'

'I'm gay,' I told her, and, for all the tears, I felt a sudden rush of relief at saying the words out loud. I'd said them to myself hundreds of times over the last few years, almost always in disbelief, but here they were now, out in the world, setting off on their own adventures. 'I'm one of them homosexuals,' I said again, looking up at her.

'You are not,' she said.

'I am.'

'Are you sure?'

'One hundred per cent,' I told her.

And that's when she started laughing. Maybe she was laughing because I wasn't going to tell Mam that she'd tried to murder me with a paperweight, or maybe she was laughing because now she had something she could hold over me. She tried to stop but the more she tried, the more she laughed. I stared at her, torn between humiliation, anger and confusion.

'What are you laughing at?' I asked finally.

'What do you think I'm laughing at? I'm laughing at you.'

I frowned. 'But why?'

'Because you're gay,' she said. 'It's funny.'

'Why is it funny?'

'Hold on there,' she said, turning away and picking up her phone again and starting to tap away at it.

'What are you doing?' I asked.

'Telling Rachel.'

Rachel was her friend. An awful dog of a girl who'd been lurking round our house for years and who always looked at me like I was a bad smell in human form. I caught her once trying on my sister's underwear when Lizzie was in the shower and she'd made me swear not to tell. She said she'd blow me if I didn't and kill me if I did. I said no thanks to both offers but never said a word about it to anyone anyway.

'Don't!' I roared, grabbing the phone off her. 'Give me that.'

'Too late,' she said, smiling.

I stared at the screen. The message was green; it was sent. *Danny's gay*, it said. *He just told me.* 'Why would you do that?' I asked, looking across at her in bewilderment. 'Why would you do that to me?'

She shrugged. 'I told you,' she said. 'It's funny.'

'How is it funny?'

'Oh sorry, Danny,' she said, sitting back and smiling

sweetly at me. 'You don't think it's funny when people text other people's secrets to each other? I thought you did.'

I had nothing to say to that and couldn't think what else to do. I just stood up and left, went back to my own room and sat on the bed and thought about Josephine Smiley and what she'd do if Joseph Smiley told her he was gay. She'd probably stop riding him, for starters.

It wasn't as bad as I thought it would be. It was worse. That Rachel lezzer forwarded Lizzie's text to everyone in our class, who in turn forwarded it to everyone in our school, who in turn forwarded it to everyone in the county. A part of me didn't care. Better out than in, as they say. But still and all, I thought it was a nasty thing to do and I couldn't make sense of it. First she tries to murder me, then she tells the world my deep, dark secret. And does anyone tell her off for it? Do they fuck. All right, she'd got it into her head that I was a bad lad and had told Mam all about Dad when I should have kept my mouth shut but none of that was my fault and even if it was, to do something like that in retaliation? It was beyond the beyonds.

In fairness to Lizzie, she seemed a little remorseful the next morning but she didn't apologize. She said nothing to me over breakfast but she kept looking over as I ate my corn flakes and finally she turned her phone off because it was practically dancing off the table with all the texts she was getting. And then later, she watched as all the lads made a laugh of me in school and she didn't open her mouth once to defend me. Normally I wouldn't care about something like that since I can give back as good as I get, but it isn't easy when you've got fifteen boys jeering you and another hundred out there in the corridors making kissy faces as you walk past.

Joseph Smiley came over and put a hand on my shoulder and said, 'I hear you're a homosexual, Danny. Is that right? Are you a homosexual? Are you not worried about your eternal soul?' and I didn't have an answer for him. He was hardly in a position to have a go at me with all the things he was doing with his own sister.

Someone stuck a picture of Justin Bieber on my locker with the words 'Danny loves Justin' written across it in pink highlighter and it took me three gos to get it down as there was so much Sellotape all over it. As if I'd love that jumped-up skinny minger anyway with the big wrinkly forehead on him.

Liam Wilson was particularly nasty, which was a bit rich as I'd pegged him long ago as one of my lot, and he knew that I knew, and I knew that he knew that I knew, which was what really drove him demented. We'd been at a party only a couple of months earlier and ended up sitting outside in the garden together, trying to smoke a cigarette and not doing a great job of it, when he leaned in a bit closer than was totally necessary and pressed his right leg against my left before saying 'Christ, Danny, I've an awful horn on me right now, do you ever get that way?' And then he looked right at me and smiled, and I said nothing, just edged away, for I tell you this, I might have been desperate for a bit of boy-on-boy action but I'd have preferred to ride my pillow like I usually did of an evening than get anywhere near his skanky cock. The lad looked like Worzel Gummidge after a hard night out. So he went in for the kill, of course, and made sure that I was abused by everyone with a mouth on them.

But it all ended a few days later and I was left in peace. Tommy Devlin, class president, captain of the hurling team and the fittest thing this side of Calais, was away at his granny's funeral in Donegal when all the bullying was taking place and when he came back pretty much every lad in the room piled on top of him to tell him the news. He listened to them without saying a word before walking over to my desk and staring down at me with a baffled expression on his face.

'Is this right what they're telling me, Danny?' he asked.

'It is, I suppose,' I said.

'Christ on a bike,' he said, shaking his head as he considered it. 'You're some lad. But look, fair fucks to you all the same.' And then he shook my hand before walking away and that was the end of the matter, and I knew then that there wasn't a boy or girl in the school who would dare say a negative word to me ever again or they'd risk falling out of favour with himself. And of course I was head over heels for Tommy Devlin by lunchtime, but that's another story.

It was pretty rough there for a few days before it got better again and it was all Lizzie's fault. And I swore I'd get her too one of these fine days.

The first I knew about the woman from Waterford was a text message that she sent Dad on his birthday. *Thinking of you, xx*, it said. The contact name was listed only as 'KM'. I racked my brain to think of any 'KM' who my parents knew but could think of no one. And it was hardly likely to be Kylie Minogue sending the text. I suppose I shouldn't have read it but the phone was sitting right there on the kitchen table and there was no one else in the room. I thought it might be important and, if it was, then he'd want me to go upstairs and tell him.

Dad and I weren't talking that morning because we'd had a row the night before when he found out about a bit of mischief I'd been up to and he'd said that there wasn't much more that he was willing to put up with from me, that there were days when he wondered whether there was something wrong with me in the head.

Mam had been saying for ages that I needed to see a behavioural specialist but I'd said that if they so much as parked the car outside the local pharmacy while I was in the back seat that I would take a hatchet to my own skull. That rightly shut them up. But after this row I heard Dad telling Mam that they'd been hiding their heads in the sand for too long and it was time to take action.

'I don't think he'll let us bring him,' Mam said.

'He'll do what he's told,' said Dad. 'I'll drag him there if I have to.'

'Do you think it's our fault?' she asked, putting on the old whiny voice.

I could listen to no more, as I heard Lizzie's bedroom door open upstairs and if she caught me eavesdropping she'd land me in it. She'd done that sort of thing before.

I made a note of 'KM''s number on my own phone before marking the text message as unread and later that day I phoned it from the payphone in the village. I had no plans for what I was going to say, I just wanted to know who 'KM' was and whether or not I could use the intelligence I gathered against him in some way. It was a woman's voice that answered and she was all breathless, like she'd just got through seducing the milkman's son. I could picture her, all blowsy and red-haired with make-up all over her face and lipstick on her teeth. A fridgeful of chocolates and white wine.

'Hello?' she said.

'Hello,' I replied.

'Who's this?'

'Martin,' I said, lowering my voice and doing my best to give a good impression of my dad. It wasn't bad, if I say so myself. I covered the mouthpiece a little with one hand so my voice sounded a bit muffled.

'Oh sweetie,' she said, squealing like a pig. 'I didn't think you'd be able to call today. Happy birthday, by the way. Did you get my text? Any chance that I'll see you later?'

I hesitated. I hadn't thought through what I might say when the conversation got going. I don't think I'd really believed that Dad was seeing another woman and to realize that he was surprised me a little. I'd thought better of him, if I'm honest. 'Maybe,' I replied. 'I'd say you want to see me for a bit of sex, is it?' I asked, and then there was a long silence on the other end.

'Who is this?' she asked finally, her voice colder than

before, and I hung up immediately, my heart pounding in my chest.

I walked in circles outside the phone-box for ages trying to think of what to do even though Sharon Lewis and Graham Rushe were sitting on a wall opposite holding hands and doing kisses with each other. Getting the auld shift. I must have walked around the phone-box a hundred times but I didn't get dizzy. Eventually Graham marched across the road and gave me a puck on the shoulder. 'Are you watching us?' he asked.

'Am I what?'

'Are you watching us, you perv?' he repeated. 'Me and Sharon?'

'Sharon and I,' I said.

'Shut up, you,' he said, pushing me back against a tree.

'If you hit me again I'll kick you in the balls,' I said, and he just grinned and hit me another puck on the shoulder.

'Go on so,' he said.

'I'll do it another time,' I said.

'Stop watching us, do you hear me?'

'I'll tell on yous,' I said, and he started to laugh but then just shook his head.

'Jesus, Danny,' was all he could say.

And then he turned to walk back across the road and nearly got hit by a car. Sharon leaped off the wall and screamed like she was in a horror film and Graham shouted 'JESUS FUCKING CHRIST' at the top of his voice because I'd say he fairly felt the thing pass him by and I fell down on the grass and broke my shite laughing. He turned and looked at me but he was in shock, I think, because he said nothing, just crossed back over the road, took Sharon by the hand and they disappeared off through the trees together. I'd say he was going to do sex with her.

I stayed in the village for a long time that afternoon, watching people going by, trying to decide what I should do next. I wasn't going to let Dad bring me to any behavioural specialist, that was for sure. The fact was, it was either him or me. And it wasn't going to be me. But this was all last year, of course. It's old news.

Liam Wilson, who'd tried to seduce me that time in the garden and make me his love slave, told me the news about Lizzie and Geoffrey. Liam didn't usually talk to me much because he knew that I knew his deep, dark secret while mine had already been revealed to the world and no one cared any more. I think he was worried that if anyone saw him talking to me then they'd know he wanted to kiss me and pull my pants down and touch me all over.

'Do you think it'll last?' he asked me.

'Do I think what will last?'

'Lizzie and Geoffrey.'

I shrugged. 'I don't know what you're talking about,' I said.

'You do of course. They've started seeing each other.'

I stared at him. 'Lizzie, my sister Lizzie?' I asked.

'Yeah. Did you not know?'

I looked away and felt a pain inside me because I liked Geoffrey, he was my friend and sat beside me in school and never made fun of me. I didn't like him as much as I liked Tommy Devlin, but still. Something about the idea of him and Lizzie together made me feel sick.

'You're making this up,' I said.

'I am not.'

'I don't fancy you, Liam,' I said, and his eyes nearly popped out of his head and his face went red like Blusher's. He opened and closed his mouth about a million times while he tried to think of something to say but there was nothing there – his head was empty, poor lad – and he just marched off, telling me to go eff myself. He actually said 'Go eff yourself, Danny,' because he was too frightened to say *fuck*.

I'd said that I was going to get Lizzie and I saw my chance now. It was Friday night and she was getting all dolled up, the eyelashes curled and the tiny dress on, and I knew she must be going somewhere with Geoffrey. I took her phone and switched it off so she couldn't ring to find it and I waited until she left and then I followed her into town and right enough there was Geoffrey waiting for her outside the multiplex and he gave her a big kiss right there on the street before the pair of them went inside.

I thought about going home and leaving them to it. I thought about causing no trouble. But then I remembered what she'd done to me and the promise I'd made to myself to get her and I didn't want to go back on my word. So I stayed where I was.

It was more than two hours later when they came out again and I was freezing and half asleep with the cold but I knew they wouldn't go straight home because no one ever did when they went on a date, or so I'd been told, and sure enough they didn't let me down because they didn't take the turn that would lead to our street but the one that led to Geoffrey's dad's farm instead and off the pair of them went, hand in hand, giggling like a pair of fools. I stayed a good distance from them and kept my footsteps quiet so they wouldn't hear me following them.

They made their way to one of the hay sheds and went inside, turning a light on and closing the door behind them. For a few minutes I didn't know what to do because I got a pain in my head and I thought I might have to go home and take a Nurofen Plus but then the pain started not to hurt as much so I wandered over to the shed and took Lizzie's phone from my pocket, switching it on and turning it to mute in case it made any noise. Rachel the lezzer was probably texting her to find out whether she could come over to shave their legs together.

The wooden slats weren't fully fitted together and it was easy enough for me to find a place where I could see through. I knew what I expected to see and that's what I saw – Geoffrey riding Lizzie up against one of the hay-stacks – but he was going at it good style because she was covered in hay and he had his arms in the air like he'd just scored a winning goal. Plus she was wearing a stupid hat that she'd found in the shed that said *Castlerea Farms* on it. It didn't look very romantic, to be honest.

When she got home that night, I was waiting for her in her room.

'What do *you* want?' she asked, and I had to hand it to her: you'd swear nothing had been going on at all for she didn't have a hair out of place. She looked as neat as she had when she'd left the house a few hours earlier.

'I found your phone,' I said, holding it up.

'Give it here,' she said, trying to swipe it off me.

'Hold on there,' I said, pressing *send* on the text I'd spent the last hour composing. 'Here you go,' I said, handing it across.

She stared at the screen. There was a simple message in green, sent to Rachel the lezzer. 'I have no self-respect,' it said, followed by a link to a YouTube video. She stared at it, confused, before looking back at me.

'I don't get it,' she said.

'Don't you?'

She pressed the link. The video started within a couple of seconds and I watched her as she went pale and threw the phone on the floor, letting out a quick scream that made me laugh.

'Here, you dropped this,' I said, picking it up and handing it to her.

'Danny,' she said, shaking her head. 'Tell me you didn't send that. Tell me it's a joke.'

But sure it wasn't a joke, so I couldn't say that it was. I don't tell lies.

Mam says that Lizzie is going to stay on in London now and has decided to sit for her A-levels instead of her Leaving Cert. Auntie Dolly got her into an all-girls' school near Wimbledon; she had to tell the truth about why she'd left Ireland but whoever was in charge apparently thought that she was the victim in all of this and that everyone deserved a second chance. I think she just wanted an international superstar in the school.

I asked Mam could I take Lizzie's old room as it's bigger than mine and isn't overlooking the main road. I said we could take all of Lizzie's things and put them into storage or just throw them away, maybe burn them in the incinerator, and she stopped what she was doing and just stared at me like she'd never seen me before in her life.

'Danny, is there some way that I can help you?' she asked. 'Is there something I can do? I'm your mother and I love you. I don't care about all the things you've done, I just want you to be happy. But I don't know how to help you. Can you tell me? Can you tell me, Danny? Can you tell me how to help you?'

And I just laughed because I hadn't a clue what she was banging on about. I think she must be getting the Alzheimer's because it's not me who's let her down, it's Lizzie, who's officially a slut and is famous all over the world as Haystack Girl. Five and a half million hits and counting on YouTube. They keep taking it down but someone keeps opening a new account and putting it up again. Some mischief-maker.

Dad's stopped calling over to see me but he's not living with the woman in Waterford any more. Apparently the relationship fell apart when the newspapers took an interest in her. And there's absolutely no way I can be blamed for that. But he's moved up to Dublin and isn't even talking to Mam any more. I don't know where things stand between him and Lizzie. I'd say he thinks she's great and goes over on the plane and takes her out for dinner and they go to see shows in the West End to-gether.

I've tried to make it up with Lizzie because, after all, she is my twin sister and we should be the best of pals. I can't even remember why we fell out in the first place. It can't have been because of Dad because that was his fault, not mine. Maybe it was the twenty euros she owed me (and owes me still). Maybe she didn't want to give it back. Anyway, she won't talk to me on the phone but I know she reads my emails because I write all the time and I tell her all the gossip from school. I told her how Tommy Devlin was killed in a car crash but she probably knew that anyway because it was all over the papers. I told her how it made me feel. Which was very sad. And I told her how Geoffrey is now class president and is still officially a legend for what happened on the haystack and how everyone respects him but still thinks that she's officially a slut. And how Blusher looks like his head will explode every time Geoffrey says something in class because I know he's thinking about the video, which I bet he's watched about a million times at home and wanked himself silly over.

I tell her everything I can think of, even the good things like how I got a part-time job in the kebab shop in town, but it doesn't matter what I say, she always replies with the same message:

'Get help, Danny. When you get help, we can talk. But not until then.'

She doesn't even sign it with an *xx*. Even Dad's former girlfriend from Waterford had the decency to sign her text messages with an *xx*. That's how completely horrible Lizzie is, so sometimes I don't know why I bother saying that I'll be friends with her again. If you ask me, for all the jokes we make about them, The Smileys don't have it so bad. At least they're nice to each other.

Rest Day

Hawke, a grey wolf in human form, emerged from the forest on his hands and knees, pulling pine needles from his palms. A sticky resin from the verdure clung to the top of his tunic, sending a honeyed scent towards his nostrils, a perfume that reminded him of the private gardens behind his home on Hyde Park Square where he had hidden from his father on so many occasions as a boy. He crawled through the closely packed foliage, his eyes adjusting to survey the open land before him. It was night now. He was tired and hungry. He hadn't eaten since that morning when Cole handed him a can of bully beef stolen from Westman's backpack, the meat oozing red and fatty from its metal container in a manner that reminded him of the separated skulls on the bodies he dragged across the boot-tilled mud when he was on stretcher duty. 'This is a conchie's job,' he complained, but no one listened. Westman himself had taken a bullet in the eye an hour before; his brains were still drying on his face, growing crusty in his long eyelashes, while Cole's hands were looting his supplies.

There were two cans, of course. Cole kept one for

himself, eating it greedily, a finger soaking up the blood that remained behind, mingling with his own as he sucked on it, eyes closed in pleasure. He gave the other to Hawke because he liked him. They had a football team in common and it seemed that this was enough to forge a friendship.

The bully beef tasted rotten, the juices a ghastly slime that stank to high heaven, but Hawke ate it all before throwing up in the latrines. Next to him, Oakley was standing with his cock in one hand, leaning against the wall and pissing on his boots, crying. But then Oakley was a crier; everyone knew that. He cried when the sun rose. He cried when the shelling started. He cried when the news came through that Lord Kitchener had gone down on the *Hampshire* and it wasn't as if he'd even known the man.

'You've heard about Westman then?' asked Hawke but Oakley ignored him. He didn't like to be disturbed while he was crying. He finished pissing and Hawke finished throwing up. Before leaving the latrine he told Oakley to put his cock away. 'Tidy yourself up, man,' he muttered.

Back in England, it was Christmas Eve. Perhaps it was Christmas Eve here too, it was difficult to tell. It wouldn't be like the Christmases of old, of course. *Rationing is brutal*, his mother told him in her last letter. *It makes savages of us all. Fortunately I know a man in the War Department who is a tremendous help in this regard.*

They were officially resting for a day. Staines started up a round of 'Silent Night' on his harmonica but no one was the slightest bit interested. Shilton told him to be quiet or he'd ram that fucking thing down his fucking throat.

'Here, Hawke,' said Delaney, the Irish boy whom everyone called Charlie Chaplin on account of the resemblance. 'What'd you ask Santa to bring you this year?'

'A night's sleep,' said Hawke.

'I had one of them a few weeks back. Didn't do me much good in the end. I still felt like death when I woke up.'

Why Westman had been in the forest was anyone's guess. A rogue group of Germans must have been passing through and killed him rather than taking him prisoner. Easier really. There were Germans everywhere in this part of the world. It was hard to find them though. Westman had a dog that he talked about constantly. It irritated the men. Most of them had wives or sweethearts back home but all Westman had was a dog. You'd swear that he was married to the thing the way he carried on. He'd left the dog with his parents in Canterbury. Schubert was his name.

Hawke had clean socks in his backpack and he'd looked forward to putting them on all day. Mother had sent them as his Christmas box. She'd put a stick of cinnamon in with them and he wasn't sure what that was all about. The old ones were covered in dirt and blood and stank even worse than the bully beef but for some reason he held them to his nose for a moment, breathing in the stench. He never found his own smell objectionable. The smell of the other men, yes, of course. They were animals, for the most part. But his own, no. It reminded him that he was still alive, still producing all the slime and mucus that a human body leaked throughout the day. Queenie, his old nanny, used to play with his feet when he was a child. There was something disturbing about the way she would sit him on the couch and take a couple of his toes into her mouth, sucking on them while looking directly into the boy's deep-blue eyes, the ones that his mother's friends said would break hearts one day. This behaviour carried on until he was eleven. Father caught her at it one day and gave her a slap; a few hours later she was gone. Took a job in the circus, or so Hawke was told. A few days later, Father was dead. Got run over in the street.

The clean socks were made from thick grey wool and were not standard issue. Mother had posted them to him and somehow they had got through without being confiscated. He could scarcely believe his luck when he opened the package. There was a letter in there too. Jane was engaged to a boy who was blind in one eye. His name was Harry Stanley and he came from a good family. Joseph had tried to sign up three times now but kept getting rejected on account of his age. It was only a matter of time, Mother said, before some fool believed he was eighteen, then he'd be shipped off to France or Italy or wherever they sent reckless boys who didn't know when they were lucky. Granny had died and they'd buried her next to Granddad. The weather was good, surprisingly warm for this time of year.

He peeled off the old socks, emitting an unexpected whimper as the skin and bones and muscles slowly re-laxed. He was uncertain whether this was tremendously painful or unbearably pleasurable. It reminded him of the sensation he felt if he didn't masturbate for a couple of weeks. The intensity of the delayed orgasm. Almost too much to bear.

He looked down at his feet, which didn't look like feet any more. They were stumpy things, the nails on his toes torn and rotten, blisters all over the soles, black blood seeping from scattered sores. Queenie wouldn't go near his feet now if she saw them. She'd faint or scream or do whatever it was that stupid women did when confronted by something unpleasant.

Hawke had always been brought to the funfair on Christmas Eve. A tall, thin, steel structure, painted gold and yellow, rose from the ground, around which a spinning wheel turned and ascended, rotating quickly so the people on the swings at the end of its spokes could scream and laugh as they soared in the air. A sensation of weightlessness. A fear of falling. Hawke had been fourteen when his left shoe had fallen off while he was near the top, the sky a shattered rainbow alive with fireworks. The boy sitting next to him, a boy he had never met before, had laughed because Hawke's toes were coming through his sock.

'Are you poor?' the boy had asked, and Hawke had blushed scarlet with embarrassment. 'Doesn't your mother darn your socks for you?'

He hadn't thought about this in years. It came back to him now.

He didn't sniff the new socks. They were fresh; there was nothing to bother with there. He pulled them on and put his feet back in his boots, wrapping the puttees around his ankles. Somehow, they didn't feel as comfortable as the old ones. He wondered whether he'd have more trouble with blisters over the days ahead.

Two boys, Arthurs and Crouch, started a fistfight nearby. A remark had been made. Something unkind. Arthurs punched Crouch in the nose and Crouch let out a cry as a pile of snot evacuated itself into his hands. 'You bloody bastard,' he said.

'Sorry,' said Arthurs. 'But you need to learn when to keep your trap shut.'

Hawke wondered whether he should try for a nap but it was almost six o'clock. The carol service would be starting at home now. The whole family would be there. Or what was left of them anyway. The year before the war broke out, when he was sixteen, he'd attended and Cathy Bligh had asked him whether he would walk her home on account of the darkness. There was a man about, she told him, a sex maniac who attacked innocent girls.

'You should be safe then,' Hawke said, smiling at her, and she giggled, told him not to let her father hear him saying things like that. He walked her home like she asked and tried to kiss her when they were near her house but she slapped his face and asked him what kind of girl did he think she was anyway. The whole thing had left him puzzled. Afterwards she told everyone that he tried to get fresh with her and her brother knocked on Hawke's front door on Christmas morning, spoiling for a fight.

'I'll give you a fight if you want one,' Hawke said

quietly, strolling out into the street and rolling up his sleeves, a cigarette hanging from his mouth.

'Just you lay off my sister, do you hear?' the boy responded, frightened now, out-matched. 'Or you'll get what's coming to you.'

Hawke had shrugged and gone back indoors where Jane had said the whole thing was too thrilling for words.

A dangerous hour now. If he napped, he would wake around two in the morning and probably not sleep again. No, he was better off as he was. He would sleep at nine. Perhaps half past eight if the sun went down quick enough.

The sarge walked past and asked whether Hawke had seen his book.

'Haven't seen it, sir.'

'You haven't?'

'No, sir.'

'Well let me know if you do.'

'What's it called?'

'Haven't a clue. Something about an orphan. And there's a woman in it who's awfully rude.'

Hawke didn't read much. Books bored him, although he never would have admitted that to anyone, as he wouldn't like to appear ignorant. No, sculpture was his thing. Had been since he was a child, when he liked to fashion naked bodies out of clay. He had an idea that he'd be rather good with stone or marble but had never had an opportunity to try yet. After the war, he told himself, he'd give it a go. He knew a chap back home, Bestley, whose father ran an art gallery on Cork Street. Or was

Bestley dead? Had he heard something about that? Did he go down on the *Arabis* at Dogger Bank? Well, his father was probably alive at any rate. Perhaps he'd stop by when he was next in London and ask for some advice. There might be a chap there who would give a chap lessons. Show a chap how to get started.

But reading? No, that didn't interest him much.

He decided to make some tea. Bellamy was in the mess tent, scratching away at a piece of paper with a pencil.

'Writing home?' asked Hawke.

'My missus had a baby,' replied Bellamy. 'I just got the news.'

'Well done, you.'

Bellamy stared at him. 'I haven't been home in a year.'

Hawke struggled not to laugh. 'Sorry,' he said, looking around and frowning. 'I can't find any tea.'

'I had the last of it.'

A few sprigs of holly were laid out near a satchel. Where had they come from?

He felt impatient now. That was the thing about a rest day. They came so rarely and you longed for them, but once one arrived your body was so accustomed to constant movement that it was almost impossible to slow down. The woods were nearby. He decided to take a walk. He put his helmet on and carried his rifle in case the Germans who had killed Westman were still lurking around.

'Where are you off to?' asked Sumpton.

'Delivering presents,' said Hawke. 'To all the good little boys and girls.'

It felt pleasant to walk away from the battalion, to enter the woods alone. That carol went through his head, 'O Holy Night'. He'd always liked that one. On that last Christmas Eve, a boy from two doors down whose voice hadn't broken had performed it in a solo and when he came to the part where the key changed he felt a shiver run down his spine. Music sometimes affected him like this. Mother said the carol service was the domain of boy sopranos and women now, a strange combination. *And the buffet is simply appalling*, she wrote. She was going again this year; she was probably there right now, with her man from the War Department, whoever he was. A few pairs of stockings or a bar of chocolate, that's all it took, and Mother was a young woman still with her looks. In the past, Father and Mother had always made such a song and dance about Christmas. They were like children the way they carried on. Even as a child Hawke had always thought it was a lot of fuss over nothing.

The sound of the branches crunching beneath his boots pleased him and he brought them down heavier for a while, forgetting about the Germans. Then he remembered and thought, oh sod it. He kept stamping.

Something turned inside his mind and he realized he'd had enough of this bloody war and decided not to turn back. He would just keep walking. Did people do that kind of thing, he wondered. Unpremeditated desertion? He'd taken nothing with him, no supplies, no overcoat, so everyone would be surprised. They might even assume that he'd been caught by the enemy in the forest. Westman's Germans might have got him. There was nothing to show any sign of actual desertion. Actually, he realized, this was probably the best way to do it.

He started to laugh. It was rather funny, all things considered. One minute he'd been sitting around, doing nothing, the next he was a deserter from the British Expeditionary Force. He'd known a few. Browne and Peace had made a run for it one day and been caught in each other's arms a few miles away, hiding in a barn. They were brought back and shot. The sergeant had told them to stop holding hands and go down like men but they told him to fuck off and then the bullets flew. Bancroft had been shot too but he hadn't deserted, of course. He'd put his guns down after that business with the German boy in the trench and said, 'Sorry, I've had enough of this nonsense.'

Would this mean that he would never be able to go home again? That he would never meet Jane's blind-in-one-eye fiancé? Never answer any more of Mother's letters? No, the war couldn't go on for ever, after all. It had been going on long enough as it was. But hold on, just because the war might end didn't mean that it would all be forgive-and-forget when it came to deserters, did it? Might there be an amnesty of some sort? Unlikely. He shook his head. He couldn't think about all that right now. He'd made his mind up.

The trouble was that he didn't know exactly where he was. He wasn't even entirely convinced that he knew what country he was in. He could narrow it down to two or three, of course, but it would be a tight call to pick the right one from there. Where should he go? Switzerland, he supposed. That's where everyone went, wasn't it? He could help them out along the Jura. Or just hide out on the other side of it.

The clearing before him didn't make a lot of sense. It was like a harvested field in the centre of countless acres of forest. He could walk across it but the trees on the other side might stretch on for several hundred miles. If that were the case, then he would be marching towards his own death. This didn't seem to bother him enormously and he worried that he was losing his mind. Something like that should bother him, after all.

He heard a rustling sound behind him and crouched down, burying himself in the undergrowth. A bird flew from a branch, followed by another; further along, something noisier, more cumbersome. He held his rifle out before him as he tramped through, expecting a fox perhaps or something more malevolent. But nothing appeared and he relaxed again, slinging the rifle back over his shoulder.

He walked on, glancing up at the gibbous moon, and guessed it was close to nine o'clock. Mother, Jane and Joseph would be home by now, laying stockings out by the hearth. The man from the War Department might be with them, on the receiving end of cold stares from Joseph. The servants would be making early preparations for Christmas morning breakfast. The ones who were still there, that is. He had run into William, who'd been with them for seven years, when their battalions had crossed paths a few months before.

'Hello, William,' he'd said. 'Fancy seeing you here.'

William had knocked on his bedroom door late one night when he was seventeen and asked whether there was anything he could do for him. Hawke had shaken his head, surprised.

'Not a thing, thanks,' he said.

'Are you sure about that, sir?' asked William.

'Quite sure,' said Hawke. 'Think I'll turn in now. Goodnight, William.'

It had been months before he'd understood what that was all about and when he did he desperately wanted to tell someone but couldn't think of anyone to tell. It felt as if he might not come out well from the story.

'It's Private Hinton, Private Hawke,' said William, when they met in the trenches, taking the cigarette out of his mouth and examining the tip. 'We're the same, you and me.'

He thought of goose now and roast potatoes. Parsnips, Brussels sprouts and pheasant. Mince pies, brandy butter and bread sauce. Mother asking for more wine and telling them the story of how, when she was a girl, her brother's friend had taken her on the bar of his bicycle to the church for Christmas morning Mass, a scandal from which it had taken her months to recover. Father, when he was still alive, toasting the King. The time Jane had choked on a turkey bone. The morning Joseph threw a tantrum when he finished opening his presents. Were they thinking of him now, he wondered.

Ahead of him, voices. His rifle raised again. He paused and listened, wary of German accents, harsh words, guttural sounds formed at the back of the throat. Would it be so bad to be taken prisoner? Or to be shot? He'd seen it happen so many times and it was usually over in a moment or two. It was hard to imagine that you'd feel any pain. He'd prefer it in the chest though, if it came to it. He didn't like the idea of his head being split in two. He felt uncertain which way to go; the trees were surrounding him, claustrophobic now. He marched through; he would take his chances.

McGregor, with a red hat on his head. A Santa hat. How on earth had he found this? Oakley, not crying for once, sitting still and staring into the distance. Summerfield handing around pieces of marzipan, a Christmas treat.

'Anything to report, Hawke?' asked the sergeant, and he shook his head. He'd doubled back on himself. He looked down at his boots; they had betrayed him. What year was coming up? This couldn't go on much longer, could it? It was getting ridiculous, the whole thing.

'Thought you'd done a bunk when we couldn't find you,' said the sergeant.

'Me, sir? No, sir.'

'Only joking, Hawke. Don't take everything so seriously. Have a piece of marzipan, why don't you? Summerfield, come over here and give Hawke a piece of marzipan. My mother used to make it every Christmas Eve, you know. Filled the house with the smell of it. Wonderful memories.'

Hawke took a piece and chewed on it, the flavour of almond and honey sweetening his saliva. He stepped down into the trench and continued along into one of the empty foxholes, placing his rifle beside him and leaning into the wall, closing his eyes. Sounds in the distance, across the fields, beyond the stepladders and the barbed wire, the divots and the bloodied mud. Boots dancing on the duckboards. The shelling starting, the guns firing. The noise of the men as they fell down into their lines. Christmas Eve and no rest for the wicked. He grabbed his rifle again and settled the Brodie on his head. He needed to be at ladder five. No time to waste. Rockets exploded in the sky above him, one of the greatest free light shows on earth. Better here than in a forest all alone, he decided, as he put his boot on the rung and climbed up, not hesitating as he threw himself over, stood up straight and started to charge.

It's a beautiful sight, he thought, as the land lit up before him like an entrance to another world. You don't see things like this at home.

The Vespa

His name was Tadhg Muldowney and he had a reputation in the town for rebelliousness. There were so many rumours going around about him that it was hard to believe they could all be true. Some said that he had been the cause of his father's heart attack after being caught by the police selling marijuana to seminarians at Clonliffe College. Others that he had been cast in a Hollywood film and would be leaving town soon to begin a new life of movie stardom. The most recent was that he'd mitched school one day to go up to Dublin and while he was there he'd picked up a prostitute off the streets and taken her to the Harcourt Hotel for an afternoon's debauchery. A pal of mine, a lad named William Wilson who wore a boot with a raised heel to balance out his uneven legs, told me that Tadhg was such an animal in the scratcher that the girl had been writing to him ever since and wanted him to marry her.

'He'd never give her his address,' I said, for I didn't want to believe this story, which seemed to diminish Tadhg a little in my mind. 'And sure why would Tadhg

Muldowney ever have to pay for it anyway? He's a really good-looking guy.'

'Listen to you, ya big puff,' said William, punching me in the arm, and I blushed scarlet as I told him to fuck off, for I realized that it would only take a few more throw-away comments like this to give myself away.

'I didn't say *I* thought he was good-looking,' I told him, feeling the rush of blood along my neck moving through my cheeks and up my ears. 'But that's what all the girls say.'

'Sure you've never spoken to a girl in your life. Unless you're talking about your sister and everyone knows that sisters don't count.'

What age was I when all this happened? My father had been dead a year already and Kathleen was preparing for her Leaving Cert, so I suppose that puts me at around fifteen. A rotten age or a brilliant age, depending on your character.

One rumour about Tadhg that I knew to be true was that he had been discovered drunk inside the church grounds late one Saturday night and when Father Kilburn came out of the presbytery and found him pissing on the gravestones, he told him that if he didn't stop immediately he would go straight to his parents and tell them what a scoundrel they had for a son. Tadhg had simply turned around, his mickey in his hand, and asked him how anyone could stop the flow when it had already begun. He'd kept going and pissed right on the priest's shoes. There was war over it.

There were other things too. He'd introduced graffiti

to the town and took great delight in taking aerosol cans out of his schoolbag and shaking them hard so the spring inside rattled like a cobra. There was something erotic – to me anyway – about the way he shook them. He'd fallen asleep in Mass and slipped off the bench, landing with a crash on the marble floor in the middle of the Hail Holy Queen and shouted *Fuck* out loud, the word roaring its way through the congregation and causing me to put a hand to my mouth to stifle my laughter. But it was the scooter that marked him out for pure danger, the little black Vespa that his uncle from America had bought him for Christmas and that he drove around town without a helmet, revving the engine so everyone noticed him, bipping the little horn every time a pretty girl crossed his path. No one had ever seen such a thing before and we were all envious.

Tadhg, like Kathleen, had two years on me but I plucked up the courage one day to ask him about the bike when I saw him leaning on it outside Crofty's Tea Shop, arms folded, wearing a pair of blue jeans with tears in the knees and a white T-shirt. All he needed was a black leather jacket and he would have been a ringer for your man out of *Grease*.

'I'd say she fairly guzzles the old petrol, does she?' I asked him, a line I'd been practising for weeks, trying different inflections as I recorded the phrase into a Casio C-90 tape and played it back to myself over and over.

'What's that?' he asked, turning to look at me as if he was surprised that someone so small and insignificant could speak at all.

'The bike,' I said. 'The Vespa. Does she cost a lot to run?'

'She's not too bad,' he said, shrugging his shoulders and checking his watch. A crow landed on a nearby electricity pole and I watched Tadhg's pale-blue eyes as he stared at it, his head not turning away until the bird flew off again.

'That's good,' I said, the stomach churning inside me. I got ready for the next part of my script, patting the pockets of my duffel coat and pulling a frustrated expression. This part I had practised in the mirror until I had it down. 'Do you have a smoke on you at all?' I asked. 'I'm only gasping.'

'You're Kathleen Carson's little brother, aren't you?' he asked, turning back to me.

'I'm her younger brother, yeah.'

'What's your name?'

'Seán.'

'And you're a smoker, are you Seán?' he asked dubiously.

'Trying not to be,' I said in a world-weary way. 'Doing my best to cut down. Today's been a bitch though.'

He gave a small laugh and reached into his pocket, taking out a packet of Marlboro Lights and tossing them across to me. 'Go ahead so,' he said. 'But you didn't get it from me.'

I opened the pack and took one out, tapping the filter against the box like I'd seen the lads do on the television. Not an ounce of sense in my head.

'You'll be needing a light there, will you Seán?' he asked.

I nodded and he handed me a lighter. I got the thing lit on the fourth attempt. I didn't cough though, for all of that. I held it down.

'I'm saving up for one of them myself,' I said after a moment.

'A lighter? They're cheap enough to be fair.'

'A Vespa. I thought I might drive one over to Galway. The pubs there are meant to be great. There's loads of girls in them, like. And they're all mad for it.'

'Mad for what?'

'I dunno,' I said, kicking the stones at my feet. 'That's just what I heard.'

His eyes narrowed as he stared at me; he was trying to figure me out I think, and then he raised a hand to greet someone. When I looked around, there was my sister Kathleen walking towards us, staring at me like I was something from a primordial swamp that had somehow managed to crawl out on to dry land to bother the locals.

'What are you doing here?' she asked when she got closer. 'And what's that in your mouth, a cigarette?'

'I'm just talking,' I said. 'And yeah. Ten out of ten for observation.' I looked at Tadhg, hoping he'd take my side and laugh, but his face was stony.

'Did you give him that thing?' she asked, turning to him now.

'He asked for it.'

'And are you going to be there later when he's got his head stuck down the toilet, puking his guts up?'

Tadhg shrugged, as if he didn't much care.

'Don't be such a buzzkill,' I said, a word I'd heard on

171

Fame the week before and had been employing to good effect ever since. This time Tadhg did laugh and I felt the heart jump inside me in excitement.

'Stop acting the big man,' said Kathleen, shaking her head. 'And good luck getting the smell of smoke out of your duffel coat. Mam'll kill you when you get home.'

'Shut up, you,' I said, wishing she'd just leave me alone and stop talking down to me. I'd been planning this conversation for so long and was heartsick that she was spoiling it on me. I still had at least four topics of conversation that I wanted to bring up: football, alcohol, my French teacher and the IRA. I had lines ready about all of them, each one more provocative than the last. The plan was that we'd strike up an easy friendship and I could ask him to take me for a spin on the Vespa and let me sit behind him as we drove out the back roads, the only chance I might ever get to wrap my arms around him.

'You're lucky you don't have a brother,' said Kathleen to Tadhg, and I noticed his expression change a little, his eyes looking down at the ground, his confidence muted for a moment. I stared at her in horror, for did she not know that Tadhg *did* have a brother and that he'd been killed in a car crash a few years earlier? The story was that he'd been high at the time and was being chased by drug dealers for non-payment of his accounts. If she'd forgotten it, she made no sign of remembering now, for she showed no shame about what she'd just said. Tadhg gritted his teeth and I wondered whether, when I was his age, I would be able to grow that neat line of stubble that peeped out from his chin and whispered its way across his cheeks. He reached up to scratch it now with dirty fingernails and as he did so I saw the bicep curl on his arm, just below where the white cotton T-shirt ended, and the pale-blue vein that ran through it. How did he get it to stand out like that, I wondered. My arms were like twigs.

'So are we going or what?' said Kathleen, and I turned to look at her in confusion.

'Going where?' I asked, dragging my eyes away from him.

'Not you,' she said.

'Sure,' said Tadhg. 'I'm here, amn't I? I've been waiting long enough.'

'Right. Well come on so.'

She moved over to the Vespa and I realized with dismay that she and Tadhg had made a plan to go somewhere together, probably to the woods outside the town so they could go mad for each other without anyone seeing them.

'You're not getting on that thing,' I said. 'Are you?'

'What's it to you if I am? Go along home and do your homework.'

'Mam'll kill you.'

'Then that'll be two deaths in the family today 'cos if you say a word to her I'll stick a bread knife through your ear.'

I opened my mouth, hoping to come up with a suitable response, but there was nothing there, and when she threw one leg over the back seat Tadhg slapped her arse gently and winked at her and she grinned back, no longer bothered by the fact that he had given me a cigarette, it seemed.

'I'll tell,' I said, hoping to scare her away. It was me who was supposed to be climbing on the back of the Vespa, my face nuzzling into the back of Tadhg's head, not her.

'Do what you like, you little shit,' said Kathleen. 'Are we right, Tadhg?'

He stepped on now too and as he tossed his half-smoked cigarette into the bushes, something made me jump forward and grab the keys from his other hand. I took a step back and stared at my prize, as surprised as either of them by what I'd just done.

'What the fuck?' asked Tadhg.

'You can't go off with her,' I said. 'She's my sister.'

'Give me the keys, little boy,' he said with a sigh, as if this was simply too much drama for him at this time of the day, and those last two words stung through me.

'I'm fifteen,' I said, clutching them tightly in my fist. 'So don't call me that. And that thing is a death-trap, there's no way I'm letting you take my sister anywhere on it.'

The words were like alien sounds coming out of my mouth and I could scarcely believe that I was saying them. I wanted to be his friend, that was all. I wanted him to like me. And somehow I had found myself with the keys of his Vespa in my hand, telling him what he could and couldn't do.

He stepped off the bike now and moved slowly towards me but I held my position on the pavement, looking up at him, feeling the heart pounding fast in my chest.

Without flinching, he lifted his left hand and gave me a belt across the face with the back of it, and as I stumbled backwards and fell to the ground, I dropped the keys and he reached down to retrieve them before climbing back on to the saddle. I looked up, the tears forming in my eyes as I held one hand to my reddened cheek, and saw Kathleen looking at me with a mixture of regret and annoyance on her face.

'Tadhg, I'm sorry,' I said, the words coming out with such desperate longing that I felt embarrassed by the sound of them, but he didn't say a word or even look back at me now, simply slipping the keys into the ignition, turning it on and pulling out on to the street. From where I stood, I watched as they disappeared down past the statue of the Virgin Mary that stood at the fork of the road, her hands raised to heaven, the expression on her face suggesting that she had had enough misfortune visited upon her for one lifetime and could take no more.

I stood up, looking down at my left hand which had a red scratch down the palm from where I had landed clumsily, and turned around, hoping that no one had observed what had just taken place, but the street was quiet and if anyone inside the shops had seen, then they didn't care, for what was it, only a couple of local lads having a scrap on the street. To them, it was just a moment like any other. Quickly forgotten. Barely worth even commenting upon.

A Good Man

I had a little job to do over in Paris, a quick in-and-out number, no frills, no fuss, but Gloria lost the head altogether when I told her where I was going.

'Paris?' she said, one hand on her hip, the other pulling the fag out of her mouth and pressing it tip-down into a flower pot. Her lower lip was drooping in the same way her mother's does whenever she's annoyed about something. It's a terrible turn-off for me because I can see exactly what she's going to look like fourteen years from now when she's her mother's age. 'I hope you don't think you're going to Paris without me, Toastie?'

'It's work,' I said, turning away so I wouldn't have to stare at the mammy's lip. 'I get in Tuesday afternoon and I'm out again first thing Thursday morning. It's not like I'll be climbing the bleedin' Eiffel Tower or kissin' up to the *Mona Lisa*.'

'Are you fuckin' some young one?' she asked, marching over and spinning me around, and I gave her my innocent/ wounded expression – one that I've had cause to use many times over the years of our marriage.

'You know full well that I'm not,' I said. 'So maybe lay off the dramatics for a few minutes, love, yeah?'

She glared at me and walked back to the kitchen where she poured half a bottle of white wine into a pint glass and threw in a bit of Britvic 55 to give it a lift. She knew that I wasn't doing anything like that, of course, it wasn't my style at all, but she wasn't ready to let it go just yet.

'If I ever catch you with some young one, I'll cut your bleedin' balls off,' she said.

'I better make sure you never catch me then, better'nt I?' I said, grinning away like a mad thing.

'Shut up, you,' she said, a half-smile on her face now as she looked out the window into the garden where the three dogs were all staring at each other in some mad Mexican stand-off. 'I never get to go anywhere,' she added, guzzling down the vino.

'Are you joking me?' I asked. 'What about when you took off with your sister to the Canaries for ten days in January? And then over to London with that Sharon one for a long weekend in April.'

'I never get to go anywhere with *you*, Toastie,' she said, mooching up to me now and setting the glass down on the counter so she could wrap her arms around my waist. She ran her hands down my sides and I could feel the way they pressed into the fat above my hips. I deffo need to lose a bit of weight. I keep telling myself that I'll get one of those personal trainers but I never do anything about it. You get all these young ones doing it now in the gyms and they're only gorgeous in their Lycra and their little bra-tops.

'We'll get a break before the end of the year,' I told her.

'Do you promise?'

'I do.'

'Where will we go?'

'Anywhere you like,' I said. 'Within reason. Wexford, maybe.'

'Fuck off,' she said. 'I've always wanted to see Venice.'

'Right so,' I told her. 'We'll go to Venice. I'll take the car.'

'We can leave Charlie with me mam. He'd enjoy that.'

'Or we could take him with us,' I said, because I knew rightly that the young lad would go mental if he was left behind. Whenever he stays with his granny she forces him out to Mass in the morning and makes him kneel and say his prayers when the Angelus comes on the telly.

'Ah Toastie, he'd only ruin it on us,' said Gloria, which made me give her a look. Maternal love, wha'? 'We wouldn't be able to go out at nights. We'd need a baby-sitter. And I wouldn't trust a foreign bird to look after him, would you? Most kids that go off to the Continent get kidnapped and sold on to the sex traffickers.'

We left it at that for now and I got my bags packed and headed off to the airport a few days later. Mary-Lou had booked me on RyanAir – *on RyanFuckin'Air* when I have made it clear on any number of occasions in the past that I don't *do* RyanFuckin'Air – so I was already in a bad mood when I squashed myself into the seat, fifty euros lighter for wearing the wrong colour shirt on a Tuesday or whatever it was they found a way to charge me for. And then there was the bus into the city from Beauvais, which takes about a hundred and twenty hours. A child behind me kept kicking the seat all the way there and I turned around to give him the daggers before asking his mother would she not do something about him.

'He's only five,' she said, as if this excused everything. She was all done up to the nines, acting dead posh. If she was all that posh, she'd have been getting off the plane in Charles de Gaulle and not in fuckin' Beauvais.

'I don't care if he's still a foetus,' I told her. 'He's giving me a sore back with the kicking. Would you put a stop to it, please?'

'Jasper, there's a good boy,' she said, patting his knee while playing some game designed for five-year-olds on her phone. He kept kicking and I couldn't be arsed starting an argument, so I got up and moved. I found an empty seat next to a quiet little nun. She was wearing some gorgeous perfume and I kept trying to get a sniff of her. She gave me some quare looks, so she did. She wasn't bad-looking either for a nun.

Thankfully the hotel was more than up to scratch. A good big room with one of those massive showers in the bathroom with a huge head on it and a narrow yoke you can pull out of the wall to wash the crack of your arse. I gave myself a great wash, scrubbing all of RyanAir's scum from my skin, and came out of it feeling like a million euros. Taking the laptop out I said a silent prayer like I always do in hotel rooms that the Wi-Fi would work. God must have heard me because it connected without a bother. I checked my regular emails. Nothing special there. The usual shite. The ma looking for a cost-of-living increase in her allowance. Sky wanting to sell me the football channels. Then I checked my work emails and the details I needed for the next day were all there in a single message.

I went out for a bit of lunch and afterwards took the 6 metro to the 7th arrondissement and strolled down the Avenue Charles Floquet, counting off the numbers on the doors till I found the one I wanted. A woman answered. She would have been gorgeous about ten years before, I'd say, but now her best days were behind her. She looked me up and down like she was deciding whether or not to eat me. I didn't know what she was expecting. It wasn't a shag, that's for sure. I'm gone to seed long since. She said something in French and beckoned me upstairs where she gave me the case, and I said, 'Au revoir, chérie,' and left.

Straight back to the hotel then, where I hid the goods under the mattress before hitting the town for a slap-up meal and a few beers. Back in my room later, I tried to work on my *Middlemarch* essay but it was going nowhere. It had to be submitted in less than two weeks and I still had about three thousand words to get down but nothing was coming so I put it aside for now. The few drinks were slowing me down, that was the problem. I got into the bed – huge it was, and soft and deep – and rolled over and that was me for the evening. Goodnight Saigon.

The next morning there was a motorbike parked across the street from the hotel for me with the keys waiting under the hubcap of the front wheel. There were a few tears in the seat with the stuffing peeping out and I felt a bit insulted to be offered something like this – is there no respect any more? – but I took her for a spin around the block and she went like good-oh, so I didn't worry. She'd do fine. I prefer not to complain if I don't have to.

I had a bit of breakfast, a whole plate of those cold meats and cheeses that they leave out in European hotels like they're having their tea first thing in the morning. There was a bottle of champagne in the centre of the buffet in an ice bucket and I wondered what kind of yahoo you'd have to be to start drinking Moët and Chandon at this time of the day. After that I buckled down to Dorothea Brooke for a couple more hours. By the time I finished I had four thousand words on the page. Clap, clap, Toastie. Nice one. Well done. Only another thousand to go and I'd be on the home straight.

There was great weather in Paris that morning and I went online again to check my route, even though I'd memorized it carefully over the previous days. I have a very good sense of direction, if I say so myself, and once I study a map for long enough I can be in a strange city and know that I'll get along fine. Not that Paris is strange to me. I've been there often. The first time was when I was a young lad and I came over for a bit of dirt with a young one I was seeing at the time. And of course I'd had a few jobs there over the last five years, so I was a bit of an old hand with the place.

I'd planned on taking a slightly longer route though, so I could ride down the western end of the Champs-Élysées and take a spin around the Arc de Triomphe. The traffic in Paris can be a nightmare but I'm a careful driver and I've never had an accident in my life. And in the end I even pulled in for a few minutes to get a squizz at the Tomb of the Unknown Soldier until one of the *gendarmes* told me to get back on the bike or he'd have it taken away.

Then back over to the financial district, keeping a close eye on the time. The job was scheduled to take place a few minutes after one o'clock. I parked at the end of the street and waited until I saw two men emerging from the bank, and then I put the old visor down, copped the big bald noggin on the fella I was after, drove down casual as you like, turning only to put one in his head and one in his heart, and the poor fucker sank to the ground while his companion just stared, not knowing what was after happening. Then I drove on, not pulling over for ten minutes, at which point I took the case from the carrier, put the gun back inside and threw the whole thing in the Seine before making my way back to the hotel where I had a bit of a snooze before dinner.

The next morning, I didn't take any chances and sat in the back seat of the bus to Beauvais so no little brat could be kicking me. Although in fairness my body felt in great condition after the great sleeps I'd had in the hotel. I thought maybe I should take Gloria to Paris after all. Instead of Venice, like.

The young lad got into trouble for fighting at school and Gloria and I were called in to see his teacher. A tall, lanky streak of misery who goes by the name of Mr Chops, which in my book is the funniest name ever. He asked whether we were having any difficulties at home.

'The washing machine's been playing up,' I told him. 'You have to put the spin cycle on twice or the clothes come out soaking.'

'And one of the smoke alarms keeps going off,' said Gloria, nodding her head so furiously that her jewellery rattled.

'Yeah, the smoke alarm,' I agreed. 'The one on the landing. Doesn't matter how often I change the batteries. It's just bip-bip-bip all the time. Does my head in.'

Mr Chops smiled and looked down at a piece of paper in front of him and examined it carefully for a bit. I don't know why he was doing that. It was just a list of books with 'Second Year Required Reading' written across the top of it. Was he smirking? I think he was. He'd want to watch that, I thought. Gloria's phone pinged and she took it out and read the message.

'Fuck me,' she said. 'Sharon's only gone and broken up with Tommy.'

'I'm sorry to hear that,' I said. Not because I thought they were a good couple – they weren't: she was an alco and he liked jazz music – but because she'd be around ours later with four bottles of wine and the watery eyes and her and Gloria would be sitting around the kitchen island all night giving it the old boo-hoo-hoo.

'Mr and Mrs Hughes,' said Mr Chops.

'It's Toastie,' I said, smiling. 'Toastie and Gloria.'

'Charles has been displaying some anti-social tendencies of late.'

'Who's Charles?' I asked, giving him the full whiteners.

'He means Charlie,' said Gloria, hitting me a puck on the arm.

'Ah right,' said I. 'Would you mind calling him Charlie, Mr Chops?' I asked. 'On account of that's what his name is, like. Calling him Charles just makes it seem like you want to turn him into someone else. He's not the Prince of Wales, you know.'

'Oh, I love him,' said Gloria, leaning forward in the seat and smiling. 'He gets a terrible bad press sometimes but I think he seems a lot happier these days, don't you? Since he married Camilla? I never thought that Diana one was right for him.'

'Sure if she wasn't throwing herself down the stairs at Sandringham she had her head stuck halfway down a toilet at Balmoral,' I said.

'That's no way to live, is it?' asked Gloria.

'Charlie, then,' said Mr Chops, interrupting us. 'He was always a good boy in the past.'

'Ah thanks,' said Gloria, beaming at him. 'We've always been proud of him.'

'But lately,' continued himself, 'he has shown a tendency towards aggression. He started a fight with Louis Walsh in the playground and punched him in the face.'

'Is there a man, woman or child in this country who doesn't want to punch Louis Walsh in the face?' I asked. 'I'd offer a reward to anyone who knocked him out cold.'

'Please, Mr Hughes,' he said, sighing. 'This isn't a joke.'

'Who's joking?'

'It's a serious offence.'

'Like I said, the name's Toastie,' I told him. 'Would you ever do me a favour there and call me by my name?'

'Toastie,' he repeated quietly, as if the word didn't sound right on his tongue.

'Thank you,' I said. 'You're not the best at getting everyone's name right, are you?'

'To continue,' said Mr Chops. 'There was the incident with Louis Walsh. And Damien Rice claims that Charles – that Charlie has been extorting money from him.'

'Is everyone in this fuckin' school named after famous people?' I asked. 'Do you have Daniel O'Donnell in the fourth class, Bono in the fifth and Mary Robinson in the sixth?'

'How much money?' asked Gloria.

'I'm sorry?' asked Mr Chops.

'You said he was extorting money from Damien Rice. How much?'

'Is that relevant?'

'I don't know,' she said. 'Why do you ask?'

'Why do I ask is it relevant?'

'Yes.'

Mr Chops stared at her. I don't think he knew what to think. 'And finally,' he said, ignoring her question. 'There was a fresh incident with Marian Keyes only two days ago.'

'Ah tonight,' I said, shaking my head.

'What incident is this?' asked Gloria.

'He tried to kiss her.'

'Get in!' I said, making a triumphant fist in the air. 'The apple doesn't fall far, what?'

'Stop it, Toastie,' said Gloria, giving me another puck, but I could see that she was smiling too. There'd been a time a couple of years before when Charlie was mad about show tunes and musicals and he stuck a poster on his wall of Barbra Streisand singing at Carnegie Hall, and Gloria's mam, who can be an awful oul bitch when she wants to be, asked did we think he might be a bit funny. A bit funny how, we asked and she made a face and did that downward sweep of the hand thing like it was the 1970s and we were all in the middle of an episode of *Are You Being Served?*

'Are you saying he might be a bendy-boy?' I asked, and Gloria's mam said, 'I'm not saying anything of the sort, William' – she refuses to call me Toastie – 'I'm just saying that he seems different, that's all. It's something you might like to keep an eye on.'

I told her straight out that if my son was a poofter, it wouldn't matter to me in the slightest, that he was my own flesh and blood and I would love him no matter how he turned out, even if that meant he was a shirt-lifter.

'Very modern,' said Gloria's oul' one, sniffing the air like I'd let one off, which I hadn't. But I meant it too. None of that sex stuff matters to me in the slightest. But still, it had stayed with me, that conversation, and I hoped it wouldn't be the case. Life's hard enough, you know, without all that aggro. Anyway, it was a relief that he'd tried to stick one on Marian Keyes.

'Can I ask you a question, Mr Chops?' I said.

'You can, Mr . . . Mr Toastie.'

'Just Toastie is fine,' I said.

'You can, Toastie.'

'This Marian Keyes one,' I said, leaning forward. 'Is she a good-looking piece or what?'

'I'm sorry?'

'I'm just asking, is she one of the good-looking girls or does she look a bit . . . you know, mannish?'

I leaned forward for an answer and Gloria did the same. You could have heard a pin drop.

'She's eleven years old, Toastie,' he said, blushing a little. 'She's just a child.'

'Ah but still,' I said, winking at him. 'You can always tell, can't you?'

'All I will say is that the boys do seem to compete for her attention,' he said. 'Although Charlie is the first to physically assault her.'

Gloria and I grinned at each other and for a moment I considered a high five but thought it might be inappropriate under the circumstances.

'We'll talk to Charlie,' said Gloria, picking up her bag. I suppose she'd decided that she'd had enough and was ready to go home to hear the gossip from Sharon.

'Mrs Hughes,' said Mr Chops. 'I have to tell you that if there are any further incidents involving Charlie, then the school will consider suspension. Which in turn could lead to expulsion. This is a very serious matter.'

'We know it is,' I said, standing up. 'And you're very good to bring it to our attention. We'll have a word with Romeo Beckham as soon as he gets in tonight and I'll tell him that if he lays another finger on that girl I'll beat six shades of shite out of him.'

'Toastie, no!' cried Mr Chops, raising his voice, and it cracked now as if he was going through puberty all over again. He coughed and tried to pretend that hadn't happened. But it had and we'd all heard it. 'That's not what we want at all! Physical violence is never the—'

'He's pulling your leg, Mr Chops,' said Gloria, giving me one last puck for the road.

'I'm pulling your leg,' I agreed, smiling at him.

'Oh,' said Mr Chops. 'Oh, right so.'

'Right so,' I repeated, winking at him as we left.

That evening, Charlie and I sat side by side doing our homework. The young lad was trying to make sense of quadratic equations – just as well as they're so useful once you leave school – and I was working on an appreciation of Milton's *Comus* and the masque culture of eighteenth-century England.

'What's this I hear about you fighting in school?' I asked him.

'I didn't do it,' he said. The standard reply.

'And trying to snog the face off some young one?'

He blushed scarlet. God love him, he's only eleven. He doesn't know what he's at yet, it's probably just something he saw on the telly.

'She's a slut,' he said.

'Ah Jesus, Charlie,' I said. 'I don't want to be hearing words like that in this house, do you hear me? And not about some poor little girl.'

'She's a slut,' he repeated, and I frowned and leaned in.

'Is she?' I asked. 'Why, what did you hear?'

'She'll give anyone a blowie for a Toffee Crisp.'

'Do they still sell them?' I asked, amazed. 'I used to love an ol' Toffee Crisp.' I hadn't had one in a long time although, to be fair, it'd been an age since I'd had a blowie either.

He told me what else he'd heard and it fair shook me. Did that kind of thing go on in the schoolyard at eleven years of age? I wasn't even pulling me own mickey when I was that young. But the kids, they grow up so quickly these days. I can't be keeping up with them at all.

'Why did you go back to school, Dad?' he asked me after we'd got back to our work, heads bowed over the foolscap paper.

'I'm not back at school,' I told him. 'I've told you that before. I'm at college. Adult education.'

'But why?'

'Because I want to better myself,' I said. 'And because I've always had a deep appreciation of literature.'

'Is that why there's so many books in the house?'

'It is, son,' I told him.

And then Gloria called us in for our tea and she read him the riot act and told him that if she ever got a call from that school again, that she'd hang him out the upstairs window by his toenails and give all his computer games to the poor unfortunate lad in the wheelchair down the road. She didn't hold back, she was in one of her furies, but in fairness to her it seemed to do the trick because I could see that he was taking it all in and he even had the good grace to apologize to us for the trouble he'd caused.

Fair fucks to him, I thought. My little straight son.

*

I received an enquiry regarding the dispatch of a politician from one of those Russian satellite states with a -stan at the end of it. I'll be honest with you, I wasn't sure about it at first, as I'm not political. I prefer finance, white-collar-type jobs. It's not that I don't *do* politics, I've probably done half a dozen over the course of my career, but there's just a lot of hassle involved and it's far more dangerous. I knew I couldn't say yes without further details though, so I met up with my agent, Mary-Lou, at The Mongrel's Bone. She wasn't always my agent, of course. I originally worked for her father, the Master-At-Arms, but he died of a heart attack three years ago and she took over the business from him, ousting her older brother in a spectacular coup that yours truly stayed right out of.

'How are you, Toastie?' she asked, sitting down opposite me and ordering a West Coast Cooler. I had a mineral water. I wanted to keep a clear head. She's only young, Mary-Lou, no more than twenty-six or twenty-seven, but she's got a good head on her shoulders. She looks after about a dozen of us throughout Ireland, the UK and the Channel Islands (excluding Guernsey) and no one has a bad word to say about her. She always remembers Charlie's birthday and sends him an Eason's voucher. Gestures like that can go a long way in my line of work.

'I'm well, Mary-Lou,' I told her. 'But I have to tell you, I'm not sure about this job.'

'Tell me your concerns,' she said, opening a Filofax and taking out a beautiful Montblanc pen, one of them fancy ones with the little snowflake things in glass at the tip. I've always wanted one of them myself. I dropped a fair few hints to Gloria last Christmas but she ended up getting me a Parker, like I was making my confirmation or something. 'Let me see whether I can alleviate them. If you feel you have to say no at the end of it, sure you know me, Toastie, there's no pressure either way and we'll find you something else soon.'

'I don't like politics,' I explained. 'It's not really up my street.'

'I don't much care for it myself,' she said. 'I have to turn the telly off whenever it comes on. But it pays good money.'

'Who is this fella anyway?'

'It's not a fella,' she said. 'It's a woman.'

'Ah tonight,' I said, shaking my head. Again, not my type of thing, although I've done it in the past.

'I can't pronounce her name,' she said. 'Too many letters. All those *v*s and *k*s. Here, take a look.' She whipped one of those tablet things out of her bag and I saw a copy of the new John Banville novel in there.

'Is that any good, is it?' I asked her.

'This?' she said, handing it across to me. 'I only started it at the weekend but I can't put it down.'

'What's it about?'

'A young lad riding an oul' one.'

I nodded. I liked the sound of that. I'd read a few of oul' Banville's in the past but I had to take them slow as there were a lot of carefully placed words in there. But the man was on to something, there was no two ways about that. I hadn't tried the crime ones though. I have no interest in any of that malarkey.

'Here, this is her,' said Mary-Lou, putting the book back in her bag and turning her screen to face me. 'She's the leader of the opposition. They're having free elections in a few months' time and it looks like she's going to win. Our client wants a different outcome.'

'Don't you love the way they always specify free elections in these places?' I said, scrolling down the page and reading a little bit about her. She was a sour-faced trout, that was for sure. Her husband had been killed by government forces a few years before and two of her young lads were in jail. A third was working as a dancer in *Wicked* on Broadway. 'As if someone would say *we're now having unfree elections. Everyone to the polls, please.*'

'We've had some great business with the Russian states ever since the USSR broke up,' said Mary-Lou, taking a sip from her WCC. 'Sure the Master-At-Arms did great business with some of those oli-whatsits.'

'Oligarchs,' I said.

'Yeah, them. Did you never do a job for him out there?'

'Once,' I said. 'A long time ago now. The visa restrictions were a fuckin' nightmare. I was in and out of the embassy on Orwell Road for weeks trying to get myself sorted. I swore I'd never do it again.'

'I wouldn't ask if it wasn't important,' said Mary-Lou. 'And this will be a nice little earner.'

'How nice?' I asked.

She told me and I whistled. 'That's the makings of a good Christmas right there,' I said.

'That's why I thought of you,' said Mary-Lou. 'It's a very good payday and with your Charlie getting older—'

I threw her a look and she stopped herself from going any further. This was out of line and she knew it. In fairness to her she went a little red and shook her head. 'Sorry, Toastie,' she said. 'I shouldn't have said that.'

'No bother, no bother.' I looked at the picture of the sour-faced trout again. 'Is she any good, do you think?'

'Who?'

'Herself,' I said, pointing at the screen.

'Good in what sense?'

'Good for her people. Is she a good politician or a bad one?'

She frowned and took a look at her nails. They were in need of a trim. 'Does that really matter, Toastie?' she asked. 'I'm surprised at you asking such a question.'

I nodded. She was right. I never asked things like this. It was unprofessional.

'When do they want it done?' I asked.

'Ten days' time. There's a conference in some place, I can't remember where. I have it written down on a Post-it note on my fridge but I forgot to bring it with me. I can send you the details later if you're up for it.'

'Will she not have great security with her?' I asked.

'She will. But they're all in on it. They've been paid off by the government. They'll give you a clear run at her.'

'And they won't shoot me afterwards?'

'Of course not. I have an ongoing relationship with these people. There'll be no nonsense at all.'

'And the visa?'

196

'You won't have to worry about any of that. I'll get that sorted. You can just pick up your plane ticket from me and be on your way. Or check-in online, that's usually quicker.'

'It's not shaggin' RyanAir, is it?'

'No, I took your notes on board about them,' she said. 'To be honest, I'd heard it from a few of the other lads too recently, so we won't be using them any more. National airlines only.'

I sighed and ordered a pint. 'All right so,' I said.

'You're in?'

'I'm in.'

'Good man,' she said, breaking into a smile. 'You've made my day. And the client will be thrilled. Here, let me get that now,' she said when the young lad brought over the drink. She handed him a five for the pint and a one for himself. She's a generous ol' skin, it has to be said. 'Cheers.'

'Cheers,' I said as we clinked glasses.

'Do you know, I've never been to Russia myself,' she said. 'I'd like to go. I remember my father bringing me back a snow-globe once from St Petersburg. It had the Winter Palace at the centre of it and I kept it on my windowsill for years.'

'Is this a gun job or what?' I asked. 'Or something more melodramatic?'

'Gun,' she said. 'Apparently they're shutting down the poisoning and dismemberment routines these days. Too flash. You can't go wrong with a gun.'

'It is a bit more civilized,' I agreed. 'Do you remember the time that fella asked about using a samurai sword?'

She spluttered out her WCC as she laughed. 'Jesus, what was he on?' she said. 'Who did he think we were anyway?'

'I'd probably slice me mickey off if I started waving a samurai sword around,' I said, laughing.

We could hardly contain ourselves then so ordered another round of drinks – she had a vodka and white lemonade this time – and told stories from the past about the Master-At-Arms. He was a great man. An absolute monster, of course, pure evil ran through that fella's veins, but he was a gentleman at the same time and I still miss him. He died too young, there's no doubt about it. But at least he died a natural death. When the good Lord called him instead of under the orders of some oligarch in one of those -stan places.

My supervisor, Trevor, called me in for a meeting about my coursework. He's ten years younger than me and looks like one of them Calvin Klein models. He wears one of the fanciest pairs of glasses I've ever seen and he puts them on and takes them off all the time during lectures and tutorials because he knows that it makes the girls crazy for him. Once, when I was alone in his office, I picked them up off his desk and tried them on in front of the mirror to see if they'd do anything for me. They were pure glass. No prescription at all. What kind of knobhead wears a pair of glasses that he doesn't need to wear? I tell you, I lost some respect for him that day.

'Toastie,' he said, laying out three of my essays on his desk. The first day I was in there I told him to call me

Toastie and he started laughing and now he says it whenever he can. I think he likes the sound of it on his tongue. He asked me how I'd got the nickname and I told him the God's honest truth and he went a little pale and stared at me like I was joking. I let it go; I wasn't going to be repeating myself over and over. 'I think we have a problem with some of your coursework.'

'What sort of a problem?' I asked him.

'The important thing about a third-level education,' he said, leaning back and making a temple of his hands – he looked as if he expected me to be taking notes for his biography – 'is that the student learns to think for himself. Forms his or her own opinions. Values creative thought.'

'Sounds about right,' I said.

'These are the things that are lacking in your coursework,' he told me. 'If I'm honest, Toastie, I can see that a lot of what you say in here is second-hand information. It's been copied from the Internet. There's a fair bit of cut and paste, don't you think?'

'A fair bit of what?' I asked.

'You're transposing articles from online sources and passing them off as your own work.'

'But sure I give them credit at the end,' I said. 'In the footnotes.' I was fierce proud of my footnotes. I'd found a way on the computer to put little ones, twos and threes after sentences and then put anything I wanted at the end of the essay.[1] I thought it was fierce classy altogether.

---

1. Just like this.

'Be that as it may,' he began, and I felt a rage build inside me at the words. I don't know why but I've always felt a great antagonism towards people who start sentences with the phrase *be that as it may*. It's completely irrational, I know, but there we are. It takes all sorts. I'm also not a fan of the word *albeit*. 'Be that as it may, we can't accept this from you. You're talking here about Dorothea from *Middlemarch* and you say that she is "an intelligent and wealthy young woman who aspires to do great work. Spurning signs of wealth in the form of jewels or fancy clothes, she embarks upon projects such as redesigning cottages for the tenants of her miserly and embarrassingly neglectful uncle." And so on.'

'But she is all those things,' I said. 'I've read the book.[2] She's a nice young one.'

'I know she is,' said Trevor. 'And so does Wikipedia, where those words were originally written. You've passed off the opinions of some online timewaster as your own.'

'I've done no such thing,' I said, reaching for the pile of papers. 'Look. Look here.' I pointed at my beloved footnotes. 'Wikipedia,' it says. 'The Internet. 2014.'

'No, Toastie, no,' he said, shaking his head and taking his glasses off before using his thumb and forefinger to massage the tip of his nose. This was another one of his tricks to get a ride off the girls. I think he thought it made him look intellectual. 'What we need to do is have a conversation about the proper way to write an essay. We'll

2. *Middlemarch: A Study of Provincial Life*, by George Eliot. Originally published in serial form between 1871 and 1872.

schedule that for next week perhaps. The other issue is the amount of classes you've been missing.'

'I have to work,' I told him.

'I know you do, Toastie. I know you do. We all have to work. But you knew when you signed up for this course that there was an attendance requirement and you ticked the box that said that you would not allow your work commitments to interfere with that. What is it that you do anyway, if you don't mind my asking?'

'I'm a contract killer,' I said.

He laughed and shook his head. 'No, seriously,' he said.

'I work for an agency,' I replied. 'I take on industrial contracts that occasionally require me to travel abroad for short periods of time.'

'And could you not ask your agency to let you work more at home for the time being?'

'They prefer to send us to different places, do you see. There's a lad from the Isle of Man who usually does the jobs in Ireland. I'm more mainland Europe, myself. Although once I did a job in Kuwait. Never again, let me tell you. And I recently got back from one of those Russian places with the -stan at the end of it. For some reason, I can't get the name of the place straight in my head. I wrote this piece on Yeats while I was there, actually,' I added, pointing at the third essay on his desk.

'This one is actually quite good,' said Trevor. 'It displays a lot of original thought.'

'Well the Wi-Fi wasn't working in my hotel room when I wrote it,' I told him. 'Don't you hate it when that happens? It drives me around the feckin' twist. If I hadn't been in one of the -stans, I would have kicked up a right fuss but you never know the trouble you might get into over there, so I left it alone. Anyway, I had to make it all up myself since the Internet wasn't working.'

'But don't you see, Toastie?' he asked, leaning forward and smiling at me. He picked up his glasses, took a quick glance at the Yeats paper, then took the glasses off again and put them back down before looking back at me. You big feckin' knob, I thought. They're pure glass! 'When you don't copy and paste, when you rely on your own analytical skills, you have the ability. You have lots of ability, Toastie.'

He looked so pleased with himself that I thought he was going to cream his pants. I didn't know what to say to him. What was the Internet for if not for gaining knowledge and applying it in appropriate situations? Most of my hits were helped enormously by the use of online resources to discover the best escape routes, the smartest hiding places, not to mention reporting on new advances in gun technology and surveillance equipment. Was he telling me that this was wrong in some way? It's great for the old porn too. There's some fantastic stuff on there. Caters to all tastes. No discrimination whatsoever.

'Are you having any troubles at home, Toastie?' he asked me, and I laughed.

'Ah don't be starting that old shite on me, Calvin,' I said.

'Trevor.'

'Sorry, yes. Trevor. Look, I have to try harder, is that what you're telling me?'

He shook his head. 'Not so much try harder, Toastie. You try very hard as it is, I know that. I just want you to use your brain more, that's all. Not to rely on other people's work so much.'

'Right so,' I said standing up. 'I'll bear it in mind.'

In the corridor outside I saw one of the girls from my class, younger than me, around the same age as Trevor. A good-looking piece and I knew that Trevor fancied the pants off her because he was always calling on her in class and grinning away like a mad thing, the old specs coming on and off, whenever she looked up at him. She was done up to the nines and I knew that he'd be slobbering all over her the minute she went inside.

'Are you in trouble too?' I asked, and she looked up at me as if she didn't know me from Adam. She knew me well enough. We'd been sitting in the same room twice a week for the last seven months. But of course she's a young good-looking girl and I'm a fat middle-aged man and God forbid she should extend any courtesy my way.

'Excuse me?' she said.

'With himself,' I said, nodding at Trevor's door. 'I got called in for six of the best. I have to use more original thought, he tells me.'

'Right,' she said, smiling like I was an idiot child that she had to humour. 'I mean, like, OK.'

'You mean like OK?' I asked. 'You wouldn't get a line like that in George Eliot.'

She sneered at me and took her phone out. I thought she was going to make a call right in front of me but no, she had some type of mirror application on it and she used it to check her teeth and lipstick. She was definitely going in for a ride.

'When you get in there, you should ask to try on Trevor's glasses,' I said, walking away.

'Why on earth would I do that?' she asked me.

'Trust me,' I told her. 'You'll see him in a whole new light if you do.'

Gloria wore me down in the end and I took her for a long weekend in Venice. *Aer fuckin' Lingus!* None better. But I insisted on taking the young lad with us and not leaving him with his granny. He was delighted, of course. Gloria not so much, but she put a brave face on it. And in the end there was some other young lad in the hotel who he palled around with every minute of the day. The two of them were inseparable, hitting the swimming pool and the snooker hall together, so we didn't see sight nor sound of him most of the time. They even asked could they have a sleepover together in the other lad's room, which was grand with me 'cos it gave the wife and me a bit of space. I'd never seen him so happy.

'I'm thinking of jacking in the course,' I told Gloria over two glasses of Prosecco in Harry's Bar. She'd insisted on going there. She said it was where all the celebs went and, right enough, there was your man Matt Damon over in the corner with a baseball cap pulled down over his head, reading a script and making notes all over it with a red pen, but looking up every so often to make sure that everyone knew it was him.

'The literature course?' she asked.

'Am I doing another one?'

'Don't be sarcastic, Toastie. It's an obnoxious trait.'

'Sorry,' I said. 'But yeah, the literature course.'

'Why would you do that? I thought you loved it.'

'I love the novels,' I said. 'I love the reading. I don't love the writing so much. I don't know why they can't just let us read the books and have an old conversation about them without making us write essays all the time. Is the world going to be any better for three thousand words from me on *David Copperfield*? Chances are that everything that can be said about that lad has already been said. He was born, he grew up, he met a bird, she wasn't having any of it, he met another bird, she died. Some oul' one in a big house went mad 'cos her fella binned her on her wedding day.'

'Still and all,' said Gloria, keeping one eye roving the bar in case anyone else came in. She was hoping for a Clooney, I'd say. Or a Cate Blanchett. Someone of that calibre. 'It's a great release for you.'

My phone pinged and I looked at it. It was Mary-Lou. *Call me*, it said. I made my apologies, as they say, and went out on to the canals. Pigeons everywhere. A couple asked me to take their picture. 'Away and shite,' I told them. I called Mary-Lou, who said was it right what she'd heard, that I was in Rome for a dirty weekend with the Mrs.

'It's Venice,' I told her. 'And I'm getting precious little of anything at the moment, I don't mind telling you.'

'Venice then,' she replied. 'It's well for some. I was there once with one of my fellas. Gorgeous, it was. You don't fancy a little trip to Florence while you're in Italy, do you?'

'We've only got one day left,' I said.

'I'll make it worth your while. And Gloria'd love an extra couple of days, I'd say.'

'What's the job?' I asked.

It turned out to be a banker. Someone involved with the European bailout fund and the IMF. 'No problem at all,' I told her. 'I'll do that for you for free.' She was delighted. Said she knew there was a reason that I was her number one guy. I went back inside and there was Gloria making a show of herself with Matt Damon.

'Come on, you,' I said, dragging her back to our seat and apologizing to the poor fella, who took it in great form all the same. Did you ever see those Bourne movies? Great fun but the lad has no idea how to handle a gun, that's all I'm saying. You'd think someone who understands them would have shown him how. It's embarrassing to watch.

'Ah Toastie,' said Gloria, as we sat down and ordered another round. 'You ruined my fun. Who was that on the phone anyway?'

'Mary-Lou,' I said.

'Oh.' She went fierce quiet then. She's never had any problem with my job all these years, sure doesn't it keep her in the style to which she's become accustomed, but she had some queer resentment over the fact that Mary-Lou had taken over from the Master-At-Arms. She thought it was weird. 'She's all tits and fake eyelashes, that one,' she always said, and I said, 'You wouldn't say that to her face', and she'd stuck her tongue out and told me that if I ever had a go with Mary-Lou she'd find out about it and castrate me.

'I wouldn't go anywhere near her,' I told her. 'Sure she wouldn't look at me twice anyway. She's well out of my league.'

'And what the fuck does that make me?'

'Someone who got lucky,' I said, giving her a wink.

'So if you drop out of the course,' said Gloria, shaking her head, not looking for a fight. 'What will you do?'

'What do you mean what will I do? Sure I have a job, don't I?'

'Yeah, but that doesn't take up much time. The course got you out of the house, didn't it?'

'Oh right. And that's what you want, is it? Me out of the house. Do you have some young lad coming round when I'm not there?'

'Chance would be a fine thing. But you know what I mean, Toastie. It gave you an outside interest.'

I nodded. I had a notion that I could just go somewhere every day and read at my leisure instead. Just enjoy the books. Set one aside if I thought it was shite and not have to get all the way to the end. Life's too short, you know?

'I'll think about it,' I said. 'Maybe I'll stick it out. I might try one more essay and if that goes down well with Calvin Klein, then I'll reconsider. Listen though, do you mind if I head across to Florence on Tuesday?'

'Why would you do that?'

'Work.'

'Oh right. And where will I go? We're supposed to be heading home on Tuesday, aren't we?'

'You and Charlie could stay on here for an extra couple

207

of days. I'll come back on Wednesday afternoon and we can fly back Thursday.'

She nodded. She didn't have to be asked twice; she loves an old break. 'You're very good to me all the same, Toastie, aren't you?' she said, snuggling up to me now because she was on her fourth drink and I knew what that meant. She'd get all affectionate and cuddly and if I could manage to persuade her back to the hotel after only one more then there was a chance that I might be given twenty minutes' attention without the need of a Toffee Crisp.

'I do my best,' I said.

'You do more than that. You take care of me. You take care of Charlie. You're a good man, Toastie.'

And I don't know why but something in the way she said that sent a shiver down my spine. Was I a good man? I didn't know. I'd never thought about myself in those terms before. In *moral* terms, I mean. This was the type of thing that Trevor had been getting at, I suppose. Using my brain, my analytical senses. Thinking for myself instead of cutting and pasting off the Internet. Not that they'd find anything there to say whether or not Toastie was a good or a bad man. I keep myself well off the radar in that sense. No social media or anything. Much like himself. The Bourne lad.

'Do you think so?' I asked.

'Of course I do. I wouldn't say it if I didn't.'

I pulled her close to me and kissed her on the top of her head. Her shampoo smelled of peaches, which was a bit unfortunate as I can't fuckin' stand peaches, the big slimy gooey things. Still and all. I looked out the window of Harry's Bar and felt a sense of well-being at the notion of Florence. I'd never been there, after all. And it was full of museums. Maybe I could wrangle an extra day out of Gloria if I told her it was grand later, that we didn't need to have the sex and we could just have a cuddle instead. She'd be so happy about that that she'd probably agree to anything. I could take a look at the paintings and the art galleries, wander in to have a squizz at Michelangelo's *David*. See the big langer on him in person instead of just in pictures.

I've always had an interest in painting, even if I can scarcely draw a straight line myself. And maybe if the literature course doesn't work out and Trevor gets on me tits too much I can switch over to art history. Roll on Florence, I thought. A new start. I might even bring Mary-Lou back a snow-globe from there. She'd love that, I'd say. She'd give me all the cultural destinations from then on.

Amsterdam

You have your first drink since your son's murder in a small bar on Amstel's curve, where the street separates from the canal and snakes its way in towards Rokin. It's the second year of the Light Festival and from where you're sitting, you can see families crossing the Blauwbrug, pausing to look at the illuminations that have sprung up on either side, the small hands of the children mittened against the cold.

On the morning of Billy's funeral, you went out to the studio room you'd built in your back garden, to the glass-fronted fridge filled with beer and wine, and reached for a bottle before changing your mind and putting it back. Although you needed something to take the edge off, you didn't want to become a cliché of a man, the type you see in a movie whose son dies, he turns to drink and before long he's an alcoholic, his wife has left him and his entire life has turned to shit. You didn't want oblivion anyway. You wanted to feel your pain. And so you haven't drunk alcohol for nine months. Until now. Until Amsterdam.

Most of the people in the bar are in their early to mid twenties, a good ten years younger than you. They're beautiful, well dressed, conscious of how they sit, speak and what they order. Their voices create a low buzz, soft-shoe-shuffling over the jazz music, and it's comforting to reacquaint yourself with a language you learned during your student days. Back then, with three years' study at UvA, you picked up Dutch quickly; your skill with languages has been helpful in your work.

A girl sitting in a corner, one half of a mismatched couple, throws you a look and you hold her gaze for a few moments. She lights a cigarette and keeps staring at you while blowing smoke into her boyfriend's face. You shake your head and turn away. She reminds you of a girl you met in a hotel bar in Geneva a few weeks ago, the sixth girl you've fucked since March. You only started cheating on your wife after Billy's murder. Before that, you had been faithful for eight years. The girl's name was Kate, or Katy. Something like that. The memory of your most recent infidelity causes you no guilt. You wonder sometimes whether you have a conscience at all. You're aware that there are people you would like to kill and you're certain that you would feel no remorse afterwards.

That first beer, a Jupiler, tastes a little sour in your mouth, so when you order another, you point towards a different tap. This one is sweeter, lighter on the tongue, and you feel a sense of calm when the alcohol starts to hit your bloodstream. You check your watch. Your wife is late – she's always late – but you can't call her, as you don't carry a phone any more. You remember when you were a student how much you enjoyed sitting in bars like this in the late afternoon with a book and a beer, watching the people coming in and out as you waited for your friends to arrive. It doesn't seem like any time ago at all. And yet if you were to stand up now and try to ingratiate yourself with any of the young people here, they would stare at you and question your motives. You're only thirty-four but you feel old enough to be their grandfather.

A boy comes over and asks whether the empty chair at your table is taken. He says it in Dutch and you answer in English.

'Do you want to sit there or do you want to take it away?'

He blinks. 'I want to take it away,' he tells you, scratching his head and smiling pleasantly. 'To sit over there with my friends.'

'I'm waiting for my wife,' you reply, shaking your head. 'Leave it alone.'

He nods and his expression shifts a little. You haven't been rude but he seems quite sensitive. You've hurt him in some way. He's a little overweight. You watch as he rejoins his table of friends and they acknowledge him briefly but because he's standing they don't involve him in their conversation. He leans in to hear what's being said but then seems to slip away from them gradually. When he takes his phone from his pocket and starts to scan through his messages, pretending to be busy, you look away and close your eyes, telling yourself to breathe. Not to lose control again.

A bell above the door sounds and you open your eyes to see Sarah walking in, dressed for the Arctic in her coat, scarf and gloves. It's December, it's cold, but she's gone over the top. She looks around and when she sees you she doesn't smile, and you get the impression that she had hoped she might have some time to herself before you arrived.

'You're drinking,' she says when she sits down, pointing at your beer.

'I am.'

'OK, that's fine.'

You smile and glance out the window, where the universe is populated entirely by people with no hold over you. A woman and her little boy are standing on the street, waiting to cross the road. She's holding his hand but after a moment she lets go and kneels down to tie her shoelace. You watch the boy, who looks like he might step out on to the road. You watch him closely. He doesn't move; he stays where he's supposed to stay. His mother stands up and takes his hand again. After a moment, they cross safely.

'Well are you going to get me something to drink?' asks Sarah.

'Sure. What do you want?'

'I don't know. Anything. You choose.'

'Just pick something,' you say.

'A glass of red wine.'

You nod but don't stand up. Your eye catches sight of her hand on the table. The veins stand out a little because of the cold. A part of you wants her to tease you by pressing it against your cheek and making you jump.

'Where were you?' you ask.

'Utrecht.'

You look at her in surprise. She had said that she was going to spend the day relaxing in the hotel. 'Utrecht? You're kidding me.'

'No. It's only half an hour away by train. I felt like seeing it.'

'What the hell is in Utrecht?' you ask.

'It's quite a pretty town, actually. I went for a walk. Saw the cathedral. Had some lunch. A boy asked me would I like to have a drink with him.'

'A boy?'

'Yes, a young barge-sailor. He couldn't have been more than nineteen.'

You nod. 'And did you?'

'Yes. He was charming. Now are you going to get me that glass of wine or do I have to go myself?'

You stand up and make your way to the bar, ordering her drink and another beer for yourself. There are photographs on the wall behind the barman. He looks like a movie star and in some of the photographs you can see him pictured with actual movie stars who've spent time there. As he reaches up for a glass, his T-shirt lifts slightly and you notice a deep scar running across his abdomen. His skin is brown and covered in dark hairs but the strip of white where the knife sliced him divides his stomach in two. You pay for the drinks and sit down.

'I don't feel like staying out tonight,' says Sarah. 'Do you mind if we just go back to the hotel and get an early night?'

'I don't mind in the slightest,' you tell her.

*

When you think about Billy, these are the things you remember:

Sarah became pregnant only seven months into your relationship and there was some question over whether or not you were the father. The two of you had not yet moved into any sort of exclusive relationship and there was another boy, a trainee solicitor, who'd been sleeping with her too. She told you both the same night, at the same time, in the corner booth of a burger restaurant, where she explained that she couldn't be sure which one of you was responsible. You were twenty-five years old at the time and felt it would be beneath your dignity to be outraged by any of this and so you discussed it calmly and agreed that Sarah would wait until after the child was born to undergo the necessary DNA tests. In the meantime, she discontinued the relationship with the trainee solicitor and said that she would like to continue to see you, regardless of the outcome of the tests. You liked her a lot; you were falling in love with her. You told her yes, of course yes, and even if the baby wasn't yours it wouldn't make any difference to you.

But as it turned out, the baby *was* yours.

You struggled during the first year of his life though, as did Sarah. Neither of you seemed capable of making any real connection with the child and you resented how he tied you to your apartment when you would have preferred to be out with your friends. It was a difficult time. You never told Sarah this but you looked into what would happen if two people decided to offer their child for adoption. You knew you would never do it but somehow it relaxed you to know the options.

Eventually, however, you grew used to Billy and things began to get better. You realized one day that you loved him. And he seemed to love you too. To your surprise, you found yourself increasingly happy and your resentment at appearing so middle class and traditional wore off.

When he was four years old, you lost him in a shopping centre. You were holding his hand but then saw a friend from your college days and released him. It was a few minutes later before you realized that he was gone. You went wild, running around shouting his name. Security brought you to their offices, where the police were called. Before they arrived, Billy was delivered back to you. He'd been discovered sitting by a fountain eating an ice cream. He had no money and you questioned how he had bought it. The security cameras revealed a hooded figure, indistinguishable, taking Billy by the hand and leading him towards the front doors before apparently changing his mind and bringing him back, buying him an ice cream and whispering something into his ear before vanishing. When questioned, Billy said that the man had simply said sorry and told him to stay there exactly where he was until he saw a guard. It was a terrifying experience and one you never revealed to Sarah. You told your son that if he said anything about what had happened he would be in big trouble and so he never did. You're not proud of this behaviour.

When he was six, you began to grow concerned about your depth of feeling for him. You needed to be with Billy as much as possible and it bothered you how beautiful you found him. Not in a sexual way, there was nothing perverse attached to your love. But you found yourself staring at him frequently, his clean, clear skin, his deep-blue eyes, the sheer elegance of his trim little body, and all you could think was what a beautiful boy he was. You hated to think of him growing older, the fluff of teenage stubble sprouting on his chin, acne on his forehead, his body beginning to smell in the mornings. The notion of him touching himself in his bed, jerking off and disposing of the evidence, sleeping in his soiled sheets, depressed you. You wondered whether you needed professional help or whether it was normal for a father to love his son this deeply.

He stole money from Sarah's purse. You saw him doing it and he did it in such a skilled way that you knew it wasn't his first time. You didn't say anything.

From the age of five until the age of seven, either Sarah or you walked him to school every morning, holding his hand every step of the way. On the day of his murder, he'd only been walking without you for a few weeks. And even then he wasn't alone. He walked with a red-haired boy named George, his best friend, who lived three doors down from you. For the first week of their independence you drove behind at a safe distance to make sure they made it there safely. They were holding hands, which moved you enormously. After that, you decided to let go. You believed he would be fine.

Once, he discovered you watching pornography on your office computer. He was standing there while you flicked, bored, through a series of images on the screen. You were fully dressed, you weren't doing anything untoward, but as one sequence of pictures changed in favour of another you saw him reflected in the monitor, a ghostly presence, and jumped. You turned to him but he wasn't looking at you, he was staring at the screen with a bewildered expression on his face. You brought him back to bed and said nothing. You went downstairs and said *Fuck* about a hundred times. You felt terrible about it, although not enough to stop looking at pornography online.

When the police told you that he'd been murdered, you started laughing. They say that the mind reacts in bizarre ways to things that it cannot accept. They didn't flinch. Perhaps they'd seen this kind of thing before. Eventually you stopped and grew dizzy and they had to help you into a seat. You asked whether Sarah knew yet and they shook their heads. At that same moment, she turned her key in the front door and came into the living room.

A few minutes later she too knew that your son had been murdered.

You prefer to travel alone these days. For one thing, it makes it easier to have sex with strangers, something you have increasingly come to rely upon since Billy's murder. You're still relatively young, you're in good shape, you're reasonably good-looking. It's not difficult to find the right bar at the right time, to dress correctly, to sit in the right seat, to read a newspaper or work on one of your columns until the right girl comes in. The Internet will tell you everything you need to know about pick-up joints. You don't go over first but you do make eye contact and you hold it. Usually, if she's interested, she will too. And it becomes obvious what's going to happen. Maybe you'll buy her a drink, maybe you'll finish your column first, maybe you'll wait for her to make the approach. You never stay the night and you prefer not to bring someone back to your hotel. You're not particularly interested in conversation but if it's something that's important to her, then you're happy to go along with it.

The funny thing is, you don't particularly enjoy it. But it passes a couple of hours and makes you feel removed from a world that allowed you, however briefly, to feel part of a family.

You were never very promiscuous when you were younger but when you look towards the future, constant casual sex is all you see and the idea neither turns you on nor depresses you. Before you met Sarah you had slept with no more than half a dozen girls and one boy. The boy was a friend of yours in college. He was in love with you, or so he said. One night you decided to let him have what he wanted. You were young, nineteen, it didn't seem to matter much to you. Also, you were mildly interested to know how it would feel, to understand what another boy would do with you, to find out where his hands, his lips, his tongue might travel. The experience didn't move you very much and you didn't want to repeat it. The boy, who had promised that a single night together would satisfy the desire that threatened to overwhelm him, only grew more attached to you, and your friendship soon came to an end. He accused you of lying about yourself. He was wrong. You weren't lying about anything. You just weren't interested, that's all. You missed him afterwards though. You'd enjoyed his company. Still, you didn't regret it.

You went back to work soon after the funeral. There were cities on your calendar, one every month or so, and you saw no reason not to fulfil your commitments. You had to earn, after all. And you liked the idea of solitude. Previously, you saw your trips as distractions away from Sarah and Billy. You would arrive, see what you needed to see, meet who you needed to meet, write your column and then be on the first flight back home to your family. For European cities, you might need only a couple of days. For the Middle East, four or five. For further afield, a week. But since Billy's murder you have been to three different continents and seven different countries, and when you visited Rome, Copenhagen, Brno and Lisbon, places relatively close to home, you spent four or five days in each one when it would have been easy to leave quickly. Sarah didn't seem to mind. Perhaps she liked the solitude too. Perhaps she was fucking someone while you were away. In your bed. In Billy's bed. If she was, you didn't mind. You felt no claims over her body.

But it was her suggestion that she should accompany you to Amsterdam.

'Why?' you asked her.

'So we can be together.'

'We're together all the time at home,' you said.

'It would be good for us,' she told you.

'I'll have to work. I won't be able to spend much time with you.'

'You will if we don't arrive at the same time,' she said. 'I'll give you a few days to get your work done and then I'll get a flight. I've never been to Amsterdam. You've told me all those stories about your time there. I'd like to see it for myself.'

It was true that you had often talked about your love of the city. The years you'd spent there had been important ones to you but somehow you had always resisted the idea of your coming here together; it was a place, a memory, that you wanted to keep for yourself. But she insisted. She said that if your relationship was to have any hope of surviving, you needed to spend more time together, to talk more, to be like you used to be. Many parents in these situations, she told you, break up within a year. Particularly when there are no other children to bind them together.

'That's not what I want,' she told you. 'Is it what you want?'

'No,' you told her. 'No, I don't think it's what I want.'

'You don't think so?'

'It's difficult,' you said quietly. 'We're going through the same experience, we've suffered the same loss, and yet I find it hard to talk to you about it.'

She nodded. She felt the same way, you knew, which was comforting.

'I don't know how two people can ever get over the murder of a child,' you said, preparing to give in and agree that she might come to Amsterdam. You were sitting in your kitchen at the time. She was drinking a glass of wine. Prior to this, she had seemed quite relaxed, quite calm. But when you said this, she picked up her glass and threw it at the wall, glass smashing everywhere, a stream of dark red smearing its way down the wall like blood.

'For God's sake,' she screamed, standing up, scaring you with her fury. You leaned back, holding up your hands to defend yourself if necessary. 'He wasn't murdered! Will you stop saying that he was murdered? No one murdered him! Will you stop saying that over and over and over and over?'

Then she left and it was very late when you heard her opening the door to her bedroom, the guest room, the room she slept in now. You still weren't sure what to call it. You were asleep in Billy's narrow bed, where you had been sleeping for months. Your own room was empty.

But he *was* murdered, that's the thing. That's where Sarah and you disagree.

You stand in a queue outside the Anne Frank House, shivering in the cold, the consequences of last night's drinking making themselves known behind your eyes. You've been here before, of course, but Sarah never has. She tells you that she read the novel when she was in school and then throws you an icy look when you point out that it isn't a novel. She stares up at the exterior of the building, the hooks extending from the gables, and runs her hands up and down her arms as she turns to look at a barge making its way along the canal. A moment later she gasps and looks at you in amazement.

'That's him,' she says, pointing to a young man dragging a rope across the deck and dropping it in a corner before rotating his arms like windmills. Despite the freezing temperatures, he is only wearing a T-shirt on his upper body and is powerfully built. 'I can't believe it!'

'That's who?' you ask.

'The boy. The . . .' She shakes her head but doesn't look away from the barge as it drifts further along out of sight. 'It doesn't matter,' she says quietly before putting a hand to her mouth and stifling a laugh. 'I can't believe it,' she repeats a moment later. Something like a groan escapes her mouth, a note of longing, perhaps. Or regret.

A party of schoolchildren are in front of you, a few years younger than Anne was when she and her family first took shelter in the annex. Twenty or so tourists are gathered behind you in groups of three or four. An American girl is chewing gum loudly, smacking it against her teeth as she talks rubbish with her friend, expressing outrage over some celebrity break-up. Their conversation is only marginally less annoying than the sound of her masticating. You turn around to stare at her and she stops in mid-flow, her mouth hanging open like some animal, the pink ball of gum attached to her lower teeth. She opens her eyes wide as if to say 'What?' but you turn back and say nothing. The queue moves forward. You go in.

The tour is self-guided and Sarah and you move through the rooms slowly, quietly, reading the words inscribed on the walls, stopping only to examine some of the artefacts or watch the video displays. People whisper to each other beneath their breath, as if they are in church, and although there is no photography allowed, you notice more than one person taking pictures with their phones. You feel irritated by their wilful disregard for the rules. The same thing happened when you visited Auschwitz, tourists pointing their camcorders into every corner of the gas chambers to record the locations of despair, despite being instructed by the guides that this was strictly forbidden. What would they do with those images, you wondered? Why would they choose to watch them upon their return home?

You feel curiously unmoved by the exhibitions downstairs. Everything is too pristine, too carefully laid out to allow you to imagine the people who lived here seventy years ago and the anxiety they must have felt. Shelley Winters' Academy Award, a touch of Hollywood in an environment of tension, seems particularly incongruous. You hear the American girl laughing loudly, like a deranged donkey, but when you glance in her direction she is dragging her friend into a different room and whispering something in her ear.

You lose sight of Sarah momentarily, then find her, then lose her again. She ascends a staircase and you follow, separated only by two small boys from the school party who seem frightened to have been detached from their group. They're holding hands as they try to move faster but the staircase is narrow and they must wait for Sarah to make her way to the top, as she too must wait for whoever is before her and so on. They let out a gasp of relief when they reach the summit and rush to join their friends. You watch them and wonder for a moment whether George, red-haired George from three doors down, walks to school on his own now or whether he has made a new friend since Billy's murder.

At the top of the house you find yourself more engaged with history. You wander through the room that once belonged to Anne, the walls decorated with pictures of film stars and the young princesses, Elizabeth and Margaret-Rose. You imagine her taping these pictures to the wall and wondering what life must be like in Windsor Castle. You assume that the Queen has visited this building at some point in her life, perhaps more than once, and wonder what passed through her mind when she discovered her own likeness there. Did she question why she had been allowed to live a long and productive life while Anne, three years her junior, did not survive her teenage years? Did she wonder which of their names would endure over the centuries ahead? You find the ordinary things almost unbearably moving – a sink, a toilet, the bookcase that hides the entrance to the annex where the Franks and their friends were hidden before their capture. Finally you emerge into a long room where pages from the diary, the original diary, are on display hidden beneath glass cases. The children march by, barely glancing in, but you lean forward to examine the handwriting – it's neat and refined – and imagine the young girl faithfully recording her thoughts and longings. You notice Sarah standing next to a tall man with a Van Dyck beard; he is showing her something in a book that he holds and she's looking at it closely before she nods and smiles at him. He says something in reply before moving on and a group of you gather before a television screen and watch as an elderly woman recounts how she knew the Franks, how Anne was once a friend of hers. She tells a story of how she brought food to the family and kept their secret. She wonders who it was who betrayed them. To this day, she still doesn't know. Her face bears an expression of incredulity that someone close to her, perhaps, committed the awful act and you wonder whether she has spent her entire life with friendship and love undermined by suspicion. You look around and think of the children – Anne, her sister Margot, Peter van Pels – confined together within these walls for two years, fearing their discovery, and a crescendo of emotion builds inside you as you consider their fate. An elderly couple with a distinctive Jewish aspect hold each other tightly and the woman removes a fine lace handkerchief from her handbag and dabs at her tears. She does it so elegantly that you are moved by this too. You can tell that she was once very beautiful and then realize that she still is. The lady on the screen is replaced by a documentary – crowds on the streets of Amsterdam, members of the Wehrmacht marching along the canals while young, handsome soldiers wave towards the camera. You watch images of Anne and her family pass by, hear of how Otto saved the diary after their capture, learn of the fate that awaited them at Auschwitz.

And then a phone goes off.

There is an audible sigh from several quarters of the room and a few heads turn, including yours. The ring tone is deafening, an irritating song designed to make people laugh, and it only gets louder as the phone is fished out of someone's pocket. It's the American girl. The one with the chewing gum. You stare at her, willing her to silence the phone, but no, she answers it. She speaks into it. She declares in a loud voice that she is in someone called Anne Frank's house, that the guidebook said they should see it, but it's like a total waste of time. She says that she's hungry. She says that she's still hungover. She asks whether someone called James has said anything about what happened last night.

The elderly Jewish gentleman walks over and taps her on the shoulder. She turns to him, outraged at the interruption.

'Please,' he says quietly, smiling a little to show that he means her no harm. 'Your phone.'

'I'm on a call,' she snaps, looking at him as if she cannot believe his audacity at speaking to her.

'Please,' he repeats, his smile fading. 'You should not do this. Think of where you are.'

'Oh my God,' she says. 'Will you *please* stop talking to me?'

She waves him away as if he's unworthy of her attention before returning to her conversation. He turns and walks back to his wife slowly, colour in his cheeks now, unable to meet her eyes.

'So disrespectful,' says his wife, shaking her head.

You stride over and take the phone out of the girl's hands in a quick gesture, no force needed. You have it in your grip before she can even realize what's going on. And then you make your way to the window, which is slightly open to let in the air, and throw it out. You would love to fling it into the canal in front of you, it would be a far more dramatic gesture, but there is not enough space in the gap for you to be able to do that. Instead it falls four floors to the ground below, where you imagine you can hear it smash into a hundred pieces. Your first thought is that you hope it didn't hit anyone.

The only sound in the room as you turn around is the voice of the lady on the television screen, telling her story once again. She is on a loop, recounting her memories over and over, day after day, year after year without end. Everyone is looking at you. Most of them are smiling. Some look anxious. Sarah is watching the American girl, who now lets out a roar of anger as she advances upon you.

'What the fuck?' she cries. 'I'm an American citizen!'

She pulls an arm back as if to strike you – you think she means to push you through the window – but before she can succeed, your hand has become a fist and you lash out to punch her in the face, striking her directly on the nose. She's knocked off her feet as a fountain of blood springs from her nostrils and she stumbles to the floor clumsily. The room gasps, the schoolchildren scatter, your former allies look at you in horror and things go blurry for you as you find yourself smothered by three or four bodies that have piled on top of you. It seems the girl has friends. Male friends. Also Americans and utterly outraged at this assault upon their blessed nation. You see Sarah disappear down the staircase as they begin their assault and your body tenses as you make no move to resist their punches.

*

Your first thought was that she must have been drunk. But it was late afternoon, school had only just let out for the day, and who is already intoxicated at three o'clock in the afternoon? She claimed that she hadn't seen him, that he'd stepped out on to the road without looking left or right, but the forensic team quickly established that this was impossible. Her car was halfway on to the pavement, after all, and he was beneath it, his lower torso crushed beneath her suspension.

You asked many questions of the doctors afterwards and they were loath to give you answers, claiming that most of it would be too upsetting for you to hear. However, you insisted. They told you that it was very unlikely that Billy would have felt anything; the car had crashed into him before he would have known what was happening. And when he was under there, in those last few minutes while he was still alive, he would have been too deeply in shock for his body to have processed the concept of pain.

An old man held his hand as he died. He was walking home from a DIY shop with a packet of light bulbs and had seen the entire thing. He was an important witness. He sat on the pavement with your son's hand in his own and told him that he wouldn't have to do any homework that evening, that everyone would understand if he took a night off. He told you afterwards that Billy said 'Daddy' over and over and that although he could not move his head, his eyes were darting left and right in search of you.

George, red-haired George, miraculously escaped injury. He'd been walking closest to the wall and the car just grazed him, lifting him off his feet and sending him crashing to the ground. As the old man held Billy's hand, as your son died, George made his way to a nearby bench and sat there weeping. No one comforted him, apparently, as they were all too concerned for Billy. This has always bothered you. You worry about George. You worry about the effect that this experience will have on him in later life.

When the ambulance arrived, blood was seeping from Billy's mouth and he was gasping for air. His eyes locked on the old man's face and you were told afterwards that his grip was very tight, tighter than one would expect from a seven-year-old boy, but then it gradually loosened and went slack as his breathing slowed down and his short life came to an end. The paramedics laid a blanket over him and attended to the driver of the car.

She was a few years younger than you, in her late twenties, but already had three children, the youngest of whom, a baby, was in a car seat in the back. When she murdered your son, she was talking on her mobile phone, chatting with a friend about an arrangement they had made for drinks and dinner the following night – a Friday – and they were coordinating their outfits. Her friend, when questioned, remembered a great deal about the conversation and, although Sarah said it was irrelevant, you asked the police liaison officer to find out where the two women were planning on going the next night and what decisions had been made regarding their outfits.

The officer shook her head and said that there was no reason for you to know any of that.

The woman tried to blame Billy at first but the murder took place in a part of the city where, by chance, a closed-circuit television system was situated and it recorded her laughing on the phone, her head thrown back in glee at the moment she sped around the corner and lost control of her vehicle. Presented with the evidence she was advised by her own representatives to plead guilty to the charge of manslaughter and reckless driving, advice that she took and which led her towards a brief prison spell and a lengthy driving ban. None of which really mattered to you very much.

And so you have a loathing of mobile phones. Of communication. Of anyone being able to contact you. If you want to see someone, or if they need to see you, there are other ways to get in touch.

Sarah has decided to leave tomorrow; you have to stay for several more days while the authorities decide whether or not to press charges against you. They've received information regarding your state of mind and apparently this will be taken into account. You are to stand before a judge early next week but have been told that you will most likely be discharged with a warning. There may be issues about your entering Holland again but you will take these as they come. And the American girl will, no doubt, pursue you through the courts for years to come, demanding millions in compensation. You already know that you would rather put a bullet in your head than a cent in her bank account.

The crowds in Dam Square are quite large for this time of year but then today is Friday and the tourists might be getting an early start on the weekend. You and Sarah agree to go for a walk together and stroll side by side but not hand in hand.

Sarah asks whether you think you would have ended up together if she hadn't become pregnant and you tell her the truth. That 'ended up' may be a bit previous. She turns to look at you and there is something approaching pity in her eyes.

'If you don't want to come home, you only have to say so,' she says, and you think about it for a moment. There is a certain freedom out there that you could embrace. You can work from anywhere. You have financial security. You are in demand from travel magazines all over the world. Why are you rooting yourself to one city and one person when you no longer have to do the school run?

'Is that what you want?' you ask her, and she shakes her head and tells you not to do that, not to turn the question around so she has to make the decision whether to stay together or separate. 'That's not what I'm doing,' you say. 'I just want to know. Would you prefer if I didn't come back?'

She tells you that she still loves you. She wonders whether she should leave her job and you should travel together. You don't mean this cruelly, but the truth is you can think of nothing worse. You would like to be young again and free of all these attachments. You tried them on, they worked for a while, they were stolen from you. You like the idea of going to a bar and reading a book without having to think that if you don't sleep with a girl that night it could be weeks before you'll get another opportunity. There's only one problem; that whenever you think of going away you still think of coming home to Sarah.

'Wait here,' she says, stepping inside a souvenir shop. She collects fridge magnets with place names of cities that she has visited and you haven't seen her buy one in Amsterdam yet. You watch her through the window, which is filled with such an extraordinary array of tat that it's like a museum dedicated to bad taste. There are other tourists inside and you watch as she peruses a wall filled with magnets, running her fingers up and down as she searches for the perfect one.

A noise to your right disturbs you and you see a little boy squealing with delight as he runs ahead of his parents before tripping and falling hands first on the cobbles. There's a moment of shock on his face as he tries to understand what has happened to him, whether he is injured, whether he needs to cry or not. You reach down and give him your hand to pull him up and he stares at you, apparently fine, before running over to his father. A knock from the window and you turn to see Sarah holding a magnet out for you to see. It shows a kissing couple in the shadow of the Westerkirk and she purses her lips at you and blows a kiss, Marilyn Monroe-style, like you were a pair of kids again and she was trying to decide between you and the trainee solicitor.

You laugh at the absurdity of the moment and she mouths something you cannot hear before walking over to the cash register and placing it on the counter. You turn. You look around Dam Square. To the right, Damrak runs towards Centraal, discharging its trains like bullets into the heart of Europe. You look back at Sarah, she's rooting in her bag for change, and you turn and make your way into the crowd, hiding within their number, advancing to the opposite side of the square.

When you feel that you are far enough away that she can no longer see you, you start to run.

Student Card

*with thanks to Bikram Sharma for allowing
me to steal his identity*

The students waiting on the ground floor of the library did not seem to understand the concept of queuing. As the line moved forward, each one tried to gain a little ground over the person ahead of them, like a restless crowd pushing forward at a boarding gate. I didn't mind. After all, I was in no hurry and if I muted my iPhone I could take surreptitious photos of girls' shapely ankles without anyone noticing. (I happen to like ankles and have a collection of over seven hundred in a folder on my computer named 'Ankles'.)

'Your name?' said the girl behind the desk when my turn arrived. She was subtly perfumed and her outfit had been assembled with the kind of attention that marks the first week, and the first week only, of term.

'Bikram Sharma,' I said, and she flicked slowly through a box containing hundreds of students' cards. 'Are they not alphabetical?' I added when it appeared that she was having some difficulty locating it.

'You would think,' she muttered, occasionally looking up from a picture and cross-referencing it with my face before shaking her head. I hoped that she would give me the wrong one, offering me the card of a boy who looked quite like me (in her eyes) for then I could accuse her of being racist and when she defended herself I would tell her that I was only joking and ask whether she might like to accompany me to the Grad Bar that evening for a drink. The awkwardness of the moment might ensure a positive response.

'Here you are,' she said finally, handing one across.

'Thank you,' I said, glad to be officially enrolled at the University of East Anglia where, as I would soon learn, twenty-nine per cent of graduates go on to incredible careers as world-famous novelists! (Or – to put it another way – seventy-one per cent don't.)

'Oh no,' I said, my voice raising as I glanced at the name inscribed across the plastic. 'Oh no you didn't!'

'What's wrong?' the girl asked.

'It's terrible,' I said, handing it back to her. 'My name is wrong.'

She looked at it and frowned. 'What's your name again?' she asked.

'Bikram Singh Sharma,' I said.

'But that's what it says.'

'No, madam, it does not say that,' I told her. 'It most certainly does not say that. Look closer please.'

She did as I asked. 'BS Sharma,' she said. 'It says BS Sharma.'

'Exactly,' I said. 'No, this will not do.'

'Am I missing something?' she asked.

'My name is Bikram,' I told her. 'Not BS. Those are

242

initials. And unfortunate ones at that. Don't you see what
will happen now?'

'What?'

'It's quite clear,' I said, feeling a prickle of perspiration
breaking out at the base of my neck. 'People will see this
card and they will not call me Bikram. They will call me
Bullshit. Bullshit Sharma.'

She started to laugh and I resisted the urge to bury my
face in my hands, which, I have been told before, is an
action which does me no favours.

'I'm sure they won't,' she said.

'I'm quite certain they will,' I replied. 'Please, madam,
if you can simply change the name on the card, all will be
well. I wish to be Bikram, not Bullshit.'

'Sorry,' she told me. 'It can't be done.'

'All things can be done,' I replied, smiling at her in a
manner that had once made a school friend of mine in
Bangalore take my face in her hands and kiss me on the
lips during mathematics class. (Later, she allowed me to
take photographs of her ankles, which were well-formed
things.) 'All things can be done if those who have the
power to do them also have the will.'

'Yeah,' she said, sounding unconvinced. 'The thing is?
The machine that makes the cards? It's not here? We get
them delivered?'

'Why are you turning these statements into questions?'
I asked, growing more frustrated. 'Speak sensibly, please.
And amend my name on this card. I will not go through
the academic year being known as Bullshit Sharma.'

'What course are you on?' she asked, sitting back now,

and despite my anger, it was hard not to appreciate her magnificent beauty.

'Creative Writing,' I said.

'Oh,' she said, pulling a face. 'You're one of them. That explains it.'

'What does it explain?'

'It doesn't matter,' she said. 'But look, there's a queue behind you, Bullshit, so if you don't mind—'

'You see?' I shouted. 'You just called me Bullshit! I told you this would happen!'

'Sorry,' she said, flushing with embarrassment. 'It's only because we were talking about it and—'

'What if I find myself in the throes of passionate lovemaking with some beautiful honey and just at the moment where the universe is exploding for her with the intensity of a million star systems colliding, a paroxysm she has never before experienced and only ever dreamed about, she shouts out, "Bullshit! Bullshit!", hears her own words and immediately her orgasm is lost? Do you want to be responsible for such a catastrophe?'

'Yeah . . .' she drawled. 'Is that likely though?'

'It is very likely. Bullshit is not a sexy term. Please, do not deprive me of my proper name. Amend the card.' A hand tapped me on my shoulder and I looked around to see a bearded student (male) tapping his watch and telling me that he had places to go and people to see even if I didn't.

'You can take this card now,' said the girl behind the desk. 'Or you can apply for a new one. But that will take six weeks to process and in the meantime you won't be able to access the library, the sports centre or any of the student facilities.'

'This is very disappointing,' I said.

'I'm sure it is.'

'Perhaps to make up for this misfortune, which is not of my making, you will allow me to ask you one more question. It concerns your plans for this evening.'

When I woke the next morning, I stretched out with the satisfaction of a man who has offered his lover untold pleasure for no less than thirty minutes the night before. My mouth was dry and as I reached across to the bedside table for a bottle of water, it fell to the ground, waking my partner, who looked across at me and yawned.

'Do you think you might be able to get my student card changed today?' I asked immediately.

'Fuck me,' she said, sitting up straight and pulling the duvet up to protect her modesty, unaware that all she was doing was exposing her ankles, which were far more erotic to me than her breasts. 'This again?'

'It's important to me,' I said. 'You wouldn't like it if you were called . . . I don't know . . . Bitch-Features or . . . or Nasty-Face, instead of . . .' I paused and knew that beginning this sentence had been a mistake.

'Instead of what?' she asked, opening her eyes wide. 'Instead of *what*?'

'Instead of . . .' I smiled at her and shrugged. 'I wanna say Harriet?'

She shook her head and removed herself immediately from my bed. I am sorry to say that in the cold light of morning her bottom was a little saggy but nothing that a daily series of lunges could not improve. Presumably *she* had a card that could access the sports centre, if only she would use it. 'My name is Gwendolyn,' she said.

'That's not an easy name to remember,' I said quietly, hoping she might forgive me.

'Bullshit,' she said.

'Don't call me Bullshit!' I cried.

'I wasn't calling you Bullshit,' she said, pulling on her clothes. 'I was saying that what you said was bullshit.'

'Bullshit,' I told her. 'You were calling me Bullshit! You can't remember my name either.'

'Your name,' she said, looking around for her shoes, 'is Bikram. Bikram Sharma.'

'Yes! And all I want is a card that reflects this fact. I don't think that's too much to ask.'

'Six weeks,' she told me, smiling sweetly. 'Re-apply and we'll email you when it's in. Probably.'

'But the sports centre,' I argued. 'I won't be able to go swimming.'

'So go running instead,' she said, throwing one last look around the room to ensure that she had collected all her belongings. 'You don't need a card for that. See ya later,' she added, waving her hand at me as she left.

I lay back down and took the card from my wallet once more, wondering whether I could simply tell people that the BS stood for something else.

Beautiful Stranger, perhaps.
Brilliant Shagger.
Bangalore Sex-God.

I could try, of course, but it was obvious what the first word out of every girl's mouth would be if I tried that.

Araby

North Richmond Street, my aunt told me, was a quiet street until I was sent to live there. Neither she nor my uncle had wanted me with them, I knew that much, but what choice did they have when my parents left for Canada, claiming that they would send for me when they were settled. My aunt showed me the box room that was once my cousin's and told me not to get too comfortable.

Jack's room was exactly as he left it on the day he wandered into the path of a number 7 bus as it made its way around Mountjoy Square towards the Rotunda Hospital. The toys and games were a little young for me, the books were ones I'd read a few years before, but I didn't mind for I felt a longing to wrap myself in the comfort of the past. I had lived in a big house before all the trouble started, when we had money, but that was gone now. People said it was my father's fault, or at least that he bore a considerable portion of the blame, and there were those who said he should be brought back from Canada to face the courts. They said he had destroyed lives and that families would not recover for generations. I scanned my uncle's copy of the *Irish Times* every morning in hope that they would achieve their goal; I wanted my father brought home. And my mother too, I suppose.

It was late autumn and the nights drew in early but I preferred to be outside than stuck within those suffo-cating walls. The house was stale; the wallpaper peeled in corners above the cooker revealing a yellow-mottled skin behind. There was a dog who was no fun, and who-ever heard of such a thing as that? My aunt sat in front of the television most of the day, drinking tea and eating custard creams, a cigarette always on the go. My uncle, a civil servant, preferred the pub after five o'clock and I didn't blame him. Occasionally they spoke to each other. A school had not been organized for me yet; they said it would come soon but the days passed and no changes happened there. I didn't mind. I yearned for company but couldn't bear the idea of having to make new friends. Boys my age intimidated me; they always had. And to be a new boy at a new school? There were few ideas more alarming.

Some afternoons, I would wander up Ballybough Road and turn right towards Fairview Park, which was big enough for me to investigate in sections. I found empty bottles of cider, small black bags filled with dog shit, Sunday supplements, half-eaten sandwiches and, once, a pair of women's underwear ripped asunder at the seam as if someone had removed them with violence. I saw a man crying on a bench as he read a letter, digging the nails of one hand into the palm of the other. I watched a boy and a girl kissing in a copse, his hand moving greedily beneath her shirt, and when he noticed me, the boy gave chase until I collapsed, panting on the damp grass, and let him slap me about the face a few times.

There was only one child living nearby, a girl of my age named Mangan, but it was her brother, a few years older than her, who caught my eye and made me hope for a protector. He went to school in a uniform but came home most afternoons in rugby shorts, his face mud-striped and wild, the hairs on his legs clay-caked to his skin.

Every morning, I watched from my bedroom window as he left the house, yawning, his bag slung over his shoulder, his tie already loosened around his neck as he put the black buds in his ears, scrolled to the music he wanted and went on his way. Then I would charge down the stairs, out the door and run after him, glad that his music cocoon prevented him from hearing me marching along behind. If he turned, he would see me, of course, but he never turned. And had he noticed me, I would have pretended not to see him at all but would have simply trotted along, ignoring him, a boy off on some piece of private business. I thought of him through the day and wondered whether he was taking notes in class, talking with his friends, changing for his match. I wondered what kind of sandwiches he ate at lunchtime and what he washed them down with.

He was on my mind constantly and it frightened me that I could think of no one else. Were boys not supposed to think of girls, had I not read that somewhere? He had thick, messy blond hair that looked as if it never saw a comb, and was stocky, like rugby players often are. How old was he, sixteen perhaps? Just a boy but a man from my perspective, a few years his junior. I saw him everywhere, both awake and asleep, and knew not why. I caught sight of him in a supermarket one afternoon, a girl walking along with him, and followed him down every aisle, my eyes on their hands, hoping their fingers would never connect. I wanted him to move away, or for my parents to send for me so that I might stop obsessing, but dreaded the notion of a *For Sale* sign going up across the street. I was as confused in my adoration as I was excited by it. I imagined what it would be like to be his friend, for him to hold me. He might hand one of his earpieces to me so we could listen to a song together, our faces close out of necessity. We would smile at each other, our bodies touching as our heads bounced in time with the music. He would reach for the earphone afterwards, his fingers grazing my cheek, and smile at me.

The gap between his front teeth. The scratch of stubble along his chin. The coloured thread he wore around his wrist. His habit of wearing runners with his school trousers. All these things were matters that I took note of and thought about, day and night.

Once, when I woke too late to see him leave, I returned to my virgin bed in my dead cousin's room and threw myself around beneath the blanket, thrashing like a wild animal, my feet wrapping the pale sheets around my ankles, mummifying myself in their whiteness as I kicked out in self-loathing and buried my face in my pillow crying out his name, spoken with longing, then with vulgarities attached, then obscenities, until finally, spent and soiled, the sheets a disgrace, I examined my thin young body and felt as alone as I have ever felt in my life, the isolation of a boy who feels that an unfairness has been thrust upon him that he will never be able to share, for who would ever understand such a thing or tell him that he is not a monster?

At last he spoke to me, asking why I never went to school. I told him there were plans in that direction but they seemed slow in coming to fruition.

'You're the lad with the father in the papers all the time, aren't you?' he asked, and I nodded, embarrassed by my father's disgrace but flattered that I had some celebrity in his eyes. 'Do you play rugby at all?'

'Not yet,' I said. 'Maybe when I start school.'

'Do you watch it?'

'On the telly.'

'Sure come up some Saturday morning to the school and watch one of our matches. Half past eleven till just before one. Lots of lads your age do. Bring us an orange for afterwards,' he added, laughing, before running across the road without even a goodbye and leaving me on the banks of the Tolka River, alone and delirious. I wanted him to take more care on the roads than my poor cousin had.

Saturday morning came and my aunt said I was to stay at home until she and my uncle were back from the shops, as there was a delivery that they were waiting on.

'Can they not leave it next door?' I asked, and she turned, annoyed by my refusal to help, and said that she didn't want to go bothering the neighbours.

'I don't ask much of you,' she snapped. 'What use are

you anyway if you won't do one simple thing after we've given you a home and food and a bed to sleep in?'

Eleven o'clock came and no sign of the man from An Post. Eleven thirty. Twelve. I could feel my stomach turning in convulsions and once, in a fit of dramatics, I convinced myself that I was going to be sick with anxiety and hung my head over the toilet bowl. I went outside and stared anxiously up and down the street in search of the van. I marched around the house, cursing all those who worked for the postal service, and banged my fist off the bedroom wall until I thought it might bruise. Finally, at twelve thirty the doorbell rang, the parcel arrived and it needed no signature at all despite what my aunt had said and I threw it on the kitchen table in a fury, grabbing the freshest-looking orange I could find from the fruit bowl, and ran through the streets towards the school where the brother of the Mangan girl played his rugby.

I was afraid that the match would be over by the time I got there but no, a crowd of a hundred people or more were gathered on the sidelines on all four sides of the pitch, a sea of blue and white for one team and green and gold for the other. They were cheering the lads on and I looked out for Mangan, whose back bore the number nine, and followed him with my eyes.

A girl was standing next to me with two boys and I listened in to their conversation.

'That's what I heard anyway.'

'It's not true.'

'It is! It happened at the party last Friday.'

'I heard he was into your one from St Anne's.'

'It was her was into him.'

'That's a lie.'

The girl turned and looked down at me and asked me what I thought I was doing, and I blushed and made my way down the field, watching as the ball was thrown from player to player, scrums were formed, lines were drawn, throw-ins were made and tries were scored. I saw the brother of the Mangan girl take the gumshield from his mouth during a break in play and watched the way his upper lip contorted as he released it, his tongue extending for a moment before diving back inside. A line of saliva ran like a wire from his mouth to the lump of plastic in his hand and only when he turned his head to the left and spat on the ground did it disappear and I felt a groaning somewhere deep inside me. He raised his shirt a little to scratch his belly and a fine trail of dark fuzz made its way beneath his navel to within his shorts; his hand followed it in for a moment as he adjusted himself. When the whistle was blown, he threw the gumshield back in his mouth and turned to run in my direction with a grace that belied his bulk, his eyes watching at every moment as the ball made its way above the heads of twenty boys and he reached both hands up, leapt in the air, dragged it into the pit of his stomach before hoisting it back with his right hand and throwing it further down the field to some shadow whose catch I did not even turn to see.

Soon, the game ended and there was cheering on the pitch. I gathered that Mangan's team had won but it had been a close thing and a good-tempered game, for the colours intermingled and there was a clasping of fists and quick hugs, hands to the back of each other's heads.

I dared to call his name as he trotted off the pitch with one of his friends, and he turned to look at me, uncertain at first before a moment of recognition made him smile.

'You made it,' he said, tousling my hair as if I was a child before running on, running past me, running away, turning to his companion and laughing about something as they disappeared back towards the changing rooms and out of my sight. I stood there as the spectators started to disperse, hoping that he might come out again. He had told me to bring him an orange and I had done so, but I hadn't given it to him. He hadn't even noticed it in my hand. Finally, a group of them emerged, an excitement of boys, pink-faced and wet-haired, talking and laughing loudly, sports bags slung over their shoulders, drinking cans of Coke and devouring bars of chocolate in one or two bites. Mangan among them, at their very centre.

I waited until they were all gone and walked slowly down the driveway, making my way back towards North Richmond Street, where I had no desire to be, the orange still in my hand. I was a boy uncertain where he was going, abandoned and left wandering in a part of the city that was unfamiliar to me, a place that would take me years to understand and negotiate.

That part of me that would be driven by desire and loneliness had awoken and was planning cruelties and anguish that I could not yet imagine.

Beneath the Earth

It was no easy task to dig the child's grave. The ground down here grows firm in the wintertime, the loam forming a solid shell above the subsoil and bedrock that pack together like hibernating animals in fear of a seasonal predator. When I was a boy, I took an interest in the land and wanted to grow peppers and sweet potatoes in the small corner of the farm that had been designated as my own but my father said the earth wasn't for wasting and I should plant crops that could put up a fight against the unremitting cold. Cabbage, he said. Leeks. Broccoli. All manner of green vegetables that I hated.

You said this was my land, I told him. To plant whatever I wanted.

Cabbage, he repeated. Leeks. Broccoli. Maybe a little spinach if you want to try something different.

I pressed my foot down on the shoulder of the spade, forcing the blade into the obstinate soil, and knew that I had a job of work ahead of me. Circling the burial ground, the desiccated trees formed a tribal boundary, their stripped branches rustling in the breeze as they whispered tales of the crime they were witnessing.

My father was long dead, of course, and the land was mine now. I could do with it what I liked. I could bury whatever I pleased inside it.

Much further away, a corner of the north field housed the grave where I had buried my wife two years before. Flynn, the priest, refused to consecrate the ground at first, saying that Niamh should be laid to rest in the church cemetery beside her family, but I told him that I was her family, that Emer was her family, and that we wanted her nearby.

Do you not think you isolated her enough during her lifetime, he asked me, without abandoning her to such a solitary resting place?

What's that now, I asked, stepping closer to him, but he didn't dare repeat the slur. I have reason to believe that Niamh sought his counsel over the years, speaking to him of matters that were private between us, a brazen act on her part that no man could excuse.

I went to the bishop on that occasion, an older man who had been a friend of my father's, and told him what I wanted.

It's a most unusual request, he said.

If it's a matter of money . . .

This has nothing to do with money, he told me, picking a scrap of something green from between his teeth and examining it before flicking it to the floor. We don't sell favours in this diocese. On another subject entirely, however, you may have seen the sign outside requesting contributions for the renovation of the episcopal house. I wonder whether you might be able to help us out with that?

I wrote him a cheque there and then.

The next day, Flynn came over with a scowl on his face and drizzled holy oil over the plot of land I had designated for the girl he tried to persuade away from me. He said a prayer at each of the four corners before standing in the centre for his final supplication while I stood nearby and smoked a cigarette, never taking my eyes off him. When she was buried later that week, he shook the incense over her coffin and speckled the wood with holy water before giving the signal for her to be lowered down. He offered not a word of condolence to me but I gave him his envelope anyway and of course he took it.

I helped fill in the ground with the excavated earth. To be honest, I was glad to be rid of her for she had been little use to me as a wife and her looks were long gone.

I had no reason to pay attention to Emer until after her mother died. Before that, she was little more than a silent, long-haired creature with a room upstairs and a habit of staring at me as if I was an ogre. Whenever Niamh did something to provoke me and needed to be disciplined, the child would run off in tears, a racket I could not abide, for her sobs would catch in her throat and make her sound like a chicken whose neck was being wrung. There were times when I thought she was a bit simple, for she almost never spoke to me, but Niamh said no, she was just frightened, nothing more.

Sure what has she got to be frightened of, I asked. If she behaves herself, she has nothing to worry about. Neither of you do.

I hadn't wanted a daughter; I knew men with daughters and they seemed to be of little use to anyone. A son was what I needed, a hard-working, obedient son, like my own father had, who would toughen up at his founder's fists. I felt irritated when she was born. And humiliated. For a time, I told no one.

Worse news was to come when the doctor, a young lad, new to the parish, said that Niamh could have no more children, that after giving birth her womb had had to be removed.

And why is that, I asked, feeling a knot forming in the pit of my stomach, for I did not like the idea of another man investigating my wife's anatomy; it was bad enough that he had been there for the birth.

I couldn't control the bleeding from the uterus, he told me.

You couldn't, could you not, I said, nodding slowly.

No, typically the womb will contract post-partum and unfortunately, in your wife's case, it was rather stubborn. I had no choice but to perform the necessary procedure. She would have died if I hadn't.

Is that right, I said, looking him in the eye, and I could hear the low growl I was making through my nostrils, like a goaded bull getting ready to charge.

At first I tried not to blame Niamh for her failings but it wasn't easy. I was still a young man and it was unthinkable to me that my entire family would consist of an infertile woman and a silent daughter who was neither pretty nor intelligent. I wanted to set her aside but the scandal would have cost me. My produce would have been blacklisted at every market fair in the province. And so the years passed, fourteen of them, and only when Niamh was planted in the ground did it occur to me that I might find another woman to give me what I needed.

I tried courting again but there was talk in the town that I had been unkind to my wife, that I had treated her poorly, and because of this the girls kept their distance. The gossips said that I hit her whenever the mood took me and that whatever spirit Niamh had once enjoyed had been beaten out of her by my fists. They said worse things too and when the sergeant came to call I told him to undertake his investigations and let me know the outcome. I have nothing to fear from you, I told him.

It's unclear how she died, he said.

Is it now, I replied.

We have concerns about your daughter, he told me.

Do you now, I said.

There was one girl, her name was Shannon, like the river, and I thought of her often, for she was a fine thing. I followed her one day down by the stream when she was walking her dog and she spun around and glared at me, her hands on her hips, doing everything she could to look strong but the expression on her face told me that she was fearful.

That's a grand dog you have there, I told her, and the mutt cocked his leg against a tree in defiance of me.

I'd say you're proud of yourself, are you, she shouted at me. The way you treated that poor girl.

You don't know a thing about it, you tramp, I replied.

We all know what you're like, she said. You're not just pig ugly but you're cruel. And if you take another step towards me I'll set the dog on you.

I laughed. Sure what was he, only a little spaniel. But still, I left her alone when I might have just taken her right there up against one of the trees and not a jury in the land would have convicted me for it.

Her father and brother knocked on my door later that night and issued threats. They said I was to leave Shannon alone. They said if I came within spitting distance of her again, they would burst my head open. The brother grabbed me by the shirt and made ready to hit me, only stopping when he saw Emer standing at the door of the kitchen in her nightdress, her hands pressed to either side of her face, her feet bare against the stone floor.

You've been warned, said the brother, pointing a finger in my face.

Word of this incident spread fast and not one of the women in town would look at me afterwards. It seemed that I could forget about courting.

I knew Luke Hartigan's father when he was a boy. We went to school together, where both Daniel and I were persecuted by the older lads. In my case the harassment took place because I'd been trained never to speak unless I was spoken to, a rule that left me shy and awkward around my classmates. Daniel, on the other hand, was despised because his father was a drunk and his mother was pure lazy. It didn't help that he almost never took a bath and smelled so bad that no one would sit next to him in class. Even the teacher wouldn't come near his seat. He moved away when he was about sixteen and I never thought about him again until he returned years later, tall, clean and good-looking. He had money to burn then and took over the dairy farm that had once belonged to his parents, running a herd of about eighty cattle, and even though every sinner in town knew how to milk a cow, he brought in machines to do a man's job.

Once, as I sat at the bar in Donovan's, I heard him explaining to a shower of fawning sycophants how they worked.

They operate by way of a vacuum, he was saying, waving his hands in the air in a manner that made me want to hit him a slap. The cups massage the milk from the teat but the pressure keeps the claw attached to the animal. It's far more cost- and time-effective than traditional methods.

Is it now, I asked, looking down in his direction and sniffing the air. Was there a stench of milk off him or was I imagining it?

Yes, studies confirm it. And your farm, he said. Might I ask what crops you plant?

Whatever I want, I told him. It's my land. I'll put whatever I want into it.

I wondered whether he had forgotten that we sat in the same classroom together thirty years before or whether he was pretending not to recognize me. Was there no trace left in my face of the boy I used to be? I paid for my drink and left without another word.

Daniel Hartigan didn't just come back with money; he came back with a wife too. An English girl. Very tall and very beautiful but given to dressing like a tart. She had a pair of legs on her and showed them off in such a way that proved her husband had no control over her.

You know your husband used to stink, I told her one afternoon when I found myself standing next to her at a market fair. She was examining some peaches for ripeness, picking them up to see how deeply the green had turned to yellow, her fingers squeezing the flesh of each one before discarding it again. She turned to look at me, startled, a colour coming into her cheeks that resembled the velvet red of the stall.

I beg your pardon, she said, her gaze resting on my teeth. She seemed fascinated by them in a way that unsettled me. I have teeth like any other man. There's nothing untoward about them.

Your husband, I repeated. I went to school with him. He used to stink the place out. He had no friends. The smell was like a mixture of stale eggs, dead bodies and piss. That's what you're curling up to when you crawl into bed with him at night.

She opened her mouth but said nothing, letting out a bark of a laugh instead before shaking her head and walking away, as if I was something contemptible, a creature whose conversation wasn't worthy of her time. That's the problem with the English. They think they're better than all of us. Even the women.

Anyway, my point is that I knew Luke Hartigan's father from way back. And knowing that the boy was the same age as Emer, I should have taken steps to keep him away from her. A time machine, that's what I need.

Before she died, Niamh made sure that Emer knew what a daughter was for. She showed her how to prepare my breakfast and cook my dinner. She trained her to iron my shirts the way I liked them and impressed upon her how important cleanliness around the house was to me. When my wife was gone, planted in the north field, I was grateful that Emer knew how to take over her chores, for otherwise I would have been forced to hire some girl from the village and I don't like strangers in my house.

In every other way, nothing much changed. She kept to her room when I was at home and almost never spoke about what she had seen on the night her mother died. Only once did she dare to open her mouth about it and I made sure that she would never make that mistake again. All in all, she was a good girl, quiet and respectful, and seemed to prefer her own company to mine, which suited me perfectly well.

Which is why it came as a surprise when I saw her standing outside the church one afternoon with Flynn, the priest, and the Hartigan boy, the three of them chattering away like a company of grey parrots. I saw the way Luke was looking at my daughter, and the pair of them only fourteen years old, and knew the thoughts that were going through his mind. When Flynn bid them goodbye and walked off in the direction of the presbytery, I held my ground and watched as they continued to talk, Emer laughing over some nonsense the boy said, Luke doing his best to ingratiate himself with her. He lifted a hand and dared to remove the pink flower from an oleander tree that had fallen into her hair and when he held it out to her, she took it, smiling, while he shifted from one foot to the other in his awkwardness. A moment later she leaned forward, whispered something in his ear, and whatever it was made him blush. She turned then and walked away, taking in the scent of the flower as she disappeared out of sight. The boy watched her go before giving a little jump in the street, his face beaming. Whatever she'd said, she had left him with hope.

It had not occurred to me that boys would one day come calling on Emer. And I knew then that I could never allow such a thing to happen. After all, my daughter belonged to me. That was the natural order of things. And no son of an Englishwoman and a once malodorous prodigal could be allowed near her. That was the day when things changed between the two of us.

Once we were certain, I banned Emer from leaving the house. There had been enough mud-slinging about me after Niamh's passing without adding to it now. Thankfully, I didn't have to insist, as she withdrew into herself anyway, spending most of the day in her room or lying on the sofa, falling in and out of sleep. Her belly grew big and her ankles swelled to such an extent that I asked her to wear slippers around the house instead of going barefoot, as those hooves of hers were ugly things to behold.

I asked her once whether there was a chance that Luke Hartigan might be responsible for her shame and she started to laugh before burying her face in her hands, the knuckles growing white as she pressed her fingers against her temples.

I barely know him, she said, a note of defiance in her voice that I chose to ignore. If I've talked to him more than half a dozen times in my life, that's as much as I can remember.

But it's not talking to someone that makes you a mother; everyone knows that. I considered various methods for getting rid of the baby but there was a risk that these could kill Emer too and I couldn't take that chance, not after everything that had happened with Niamh. The last thing I needed was another visit from the sergeant. So I decided to wait until the creature was born and act then.

Had it been a boy, I might have reconsidered. A son, a grandson, however I might have defined him, I could have trained him up to run the farm with me. Looking after two of us would have given Emer something to do, for I swear there are days when that girl just sits around bone idle, staring out the window.

I didn't let the doctor, the young lad, anywhere near her. Women were having babies long before doctors were invented and I predicted that her body would do most of the work for her without any encouragement from the likes of him. And I was right too. She started in the afternoon and I lay her down on her bed before sharpening a knife and scalding the blade in the fire for when the time came to cut the cord.

When she finally stopped screaming and the house

was quiet again, save for the mewling of the child, I went in and did my best to avoid looking at the mess she'd left behind her on the sheets. I told her she could wait until the morning when she had her strength back to wash them up and she reached towards me, arms outstretched, emitting an animal-like sound as I took the baby from her and squeezed my fingers together on either side of the infant's nose, the heel of my hand over her mouth until she went silent. Looking around as I waited, I was surprised to see a photograph of Niamh on Emer's bed-side table. I'd never noticed it before, but then every time I'd come in here it had been the middle of the night and I'd never once thought to turn the lights on.

Outside I laid the bundle on the ground while I got on with the grave-digging and then planted the little mite in the ground before filling her over. She would be warm there at least, in the dark and tightly packed earth.

They say we're going to have a good summer this year. It'll only be a few days before Emer is up and about again and then I will start my planting. I might take on a boy from the village to help me. Luke Hartigan, perhaps, just to keep an eye on him. Maybe I'll sow the seeds for the peppers and the sweet potatoes that my father would never let me plant when I was a child. He's long gone, after all, and has no say in these matters any more. The land is mine now. And by God, I'll put anything that I want into it.